Valegro

The Early Years

The Blueberry Stories: Book Two

Carl Hester MBE with Janet Rising

with illustrations by Helena Öhmark

Matador
9 Priory Business Park,
Wistow Road, Kibworth Beauchamp,
Leicestershire. LE8 0RX
Tel: 0116 279 2299
Email: books@troubador.co.uk
Web: www.troubador.co.uk/matador
Twitter: @matadorbooks

ISBN 978 1788033 473

British Library Cataloguing in Publication Data.
A catalogue record for this book is available from the British Library.

Printed and bound in the UK by TJ International, Padstow, Cornwall
Typeset in 12pt Book Antiqua by Troubador Publishing Ltd, Leicester, UK

Matador is an imprint of Troubador Publishing Ltd

*This book is dedicated to Gertjan and
Anne van Olst, and to Joop and Martje Hanse,
who own Blueberry's sire and dam, and played
such an important part in his early years*

Chapter one

Blueberry couldn't tell how many people were watching him – they were far away and their outlines were blurred, making the audience seem like a single, multi-coloured mass – but he could hear them calling his name. Not his stable name, Blueberry, given to him on his arrival at Brook Mill Stables, but his registered name. *Valegro!* The crowd chanted, waved and clapped. *'The dancing horse,'* they

1

cried. Blueberry arched his neck and felt his feet tingle as he lifted them higher, high like The Silver Dancer, higher even than the inspirational metal sculpture could achieve. This, he thought, *this* was what he had always wanted; to dance like no other horse had ever danced, to perform dressage better than the crowds had ever before witnessed, to be the best dressage horse the world had ever known...

"What are you grunting about?" The voice was far away, but insistent. "Stop twitching, you're causing a draught!"

The cheering grew fainter and fainter and the crowd faded away to nothing as Blueberry opened his eyes to find himself lying in his stable at Brook Mill, his friend Lulu, the little tan-coloured dog, looking at him crossly with her one eye as the last of the cheers faded in his head.

"Oh," said Blueberry, sighing.

"Dreaming again?" asked Lulu, a little more kindly this time.

Blueberry nodded. "It was wonderful," he sighed. "I was performing piaffe even higher than The Silver Dancer and everyone was cheering."

"Hmmmm," grunted Lulu. "I think you'll find kiddo that, when you do begin competing, things won't be quite like your dreams – not for

2

a while at least. You won't be doing any Silver Dancer movements for a couple of years. I've told you that – and as for performing *better* than The Silver Dancer, well, that would be something to see."

"I know," said the little brown horse. "I haven't been to any competitions yet – but I can't wait. When do you think Carl will take me?"

"When you're ready, kiddo, when you're ready," Lulu told him. "Now shake those wood chippings off your forelock and go back to sleep. A top dressage horse needs quality shut-eye in order to be refreshed for his work!"

As Lulu closed her one eye and drifted back to sleep, Blueberry looked up to the dark square which was the top, open half of his stable door. He could see the stars twinkling above them both, hear the occasional rustle of the other horses in the stables around him and the strange night sounds he couldn't identify – maybe a fox or a badger passing by, an owl landing on a tree or one of the stable cats on a night prowl. The leaves on the nearby trees rustled softly in the breeze and Blueberry thought back to his dream.

Some people think animals don't dream, that it is something only humans experience, but you only have to watch a dog asleep on a rug, his legs twitching, whimpering softly, to know that he is chasing imaginary rabbits, or swimming in the sea or enjoying any number of the things he loves to do, to know for certain that he can only be dreaming. Upon waking, a dog will seem surprised to find he is at home in front of the fire, before lying down again with a sigh, hoping to return to his wonderful sleepy world.

Horses rarely experience deep sleep. Mostly, they take short naps throughout the day and night, standing upright, one back leg resting, always ready to flee from predators because, even though many now live in the safety of a stable or a secure field, the instinct is still there. It is only occasionally that a horse will lie down and fall into a deep sleep and when they do, just like you and I, they sometimes dream.

This wasn't Blueberry's first dream. When he had gone back to Holland, when Carl had decided the little brown horse wasn't big enough to ride in competitions himself, Blueberry had dreamed of returning to Brook Mill Stables, dreamed of being reunited with his friends Lulu, the big dog Willow, his equine friends Orange and Uthopia and his groom Lydia and, of course, Carl. That dream had, miraculously, come true. Carl had brought him home, given him a second chance to train hard to achieve his ultimate aim; to be a top dressage horse,

4

to emulate the inspirational pose of The Silver Dancer (Carl's amazing metal sculpture lit by coloured lights) dancing forever in piaffe, the most difficult and beautiful of all the dressage movements.

If that dream – the seemingly impossible dream of returning to Brook Mill and Carl – could come true Blueberry thought, then maybe his dream to become a top dressage horse stood a chance of coming to fruition, too. The success of this dream, Blueberry knew, rested entirely with him. Only he could make it happen, together with the help of his friends. He had Carl, one of the best dressage riders in the world, to train him so there would be no excuse if he failed. The little brown horse was determined to work harder than any horse Carl had ever trained, to learn all he could and do his very best. Only this way, Blueberry realised, would he achieve his ambition.

Resting his muzzle on the snowy wood chippings, and hearing the soft snoring of his friend beside him, Blueberry closed his eyes and drifted back to sleep.

Chapter two

Since his return to Brook Mill Stables, Blueberry's world had changed completely. He remembered all his previous lessons when he had been carefully backed and ridden by Carl's trusted trainers and riders, and had continued to learn under saddle in the indoor school and outside arena – under Carl's careful instruction. Now Carl had decided the little brown horse which showed so much promise was destined to stay, progress in his education continued in earnest. Not that the training seemed arduous to Blueberry, even when he was ridden and schooled in the indoor or outdoor arena, under Carl's eagle eye.

All the horses at Brook Mill were schooled by Carl's pupils and riders who worked at the yard, as well as Carl himself. It wasn't possible for Carl to ride every horse on his yard, every single day, and his pupils and riders enjoyed riding fantastic horses and benefited from Carl's experience and teaching. They learned not just to ride all sorts of horses – from those just backed to those competing at the highest level – but they also learned how to teach their mounts, to school them in the basic training so important if they were to further their career. Then, as the horses' muscles developed and they understood what was wanted, they could progress to the more advanced movements. The greatest riders are those who can not only school horses, but those who listen to the horses they are riding and learn *from* them. 'If you want to be great riders,' Blueberry often heard Carl telling his pupils, 'learn from each and every horse you ride. Every horse has something to teach you, and sometimes you don't realise what that lesson is until years later!'

Blueberry enjoyed his lessons in the school and hearing what Carl had to say but, at first, he didn't really understand that he was actually *learning*. To him, it felt as though he was just being ridden around. He already understood that he needed to go forward when he felt his riders' legs close around his sides, but gradually his riders – especially Lucy, who often rode him now – taught him to listen for ever-quieter signals, known as aids, from their legs. It wasn't very long before Blueberry sprang forward or increased his pace whenever he felt even the slightest thought from the legs wrapped around his sides, and he slowed down and paid attention if he felt the merest vibration on his mouth from the bit, through the reins in his rider's hands.

Blueberry learned to move straight, his hind hooves overlapping the tracks made by his front hooves which, he came to understand, was very important. If he wiggled a little, or his body wasn't straight, or if his hind hooves made an impression on the sand surface next to those made by his front hooves instead of in front of them, Blueberry would feel his rider close a leg, or feel on the rein to help support him and encourage him to straighten. Gradually, he got so used to moving straight, that anything else felt strange.

The little brown horse learned how to walk, trot and canter in big circles. Just as when he was going in a straight line his hind legs needed to follow his front legs, and his body needed to curve around his rider's inside leg. If his hindquarters swung outside the circle, he felt the rider support him with their own outside leg and if Blueberry rushed, thinking he was being asked to go faster, he felt his rider sit up and close their fingers around the outside rein to steady him, and let him know which speed, or pace, was wanted. It was important that this early groundwork was carried out steadily, slowly and progressively, but to Blueberry it just seemed as though he was walking, trotting and cantering around with the other horses. He hardly realised he was being taught the vital basics of schooling, and he didn't really appreciate the attention to detail on which Carl insisted. He was learning without realising it. And because he didn't realise it, he didn't understand its importance.

"When am I going to start doing the more impressive things, like passage and piaffe?" Blueberry asked Lulu, his chin wobbling, and not for the first time. When he was turned out in the field, Blueberry forfeited some of his grazing time to watch the advanced horses trotting and cantering sideways and performing passage –

9

a hesitant trot, and piaffe – a trot on the spot – and he longed to do them with a rider, too. Looking at her friend's chin, Lulu knew what it meant. The little brown horse's chin always wobbled when he was thinking hard or worried about something. The more worried he was, the more activity in his chin. Lulu couldn't give her friend the answer he was looking for.

"Passage and piaffe are the very advanced movements, you know that," she said, looking at him seriously with her one eye. Blueberry didn't know how the little tan dog had come to lose her other eye, and he didn't like to ask. It never seemed to worry her much – and it certainly didn't slow her down in any way. She always billed herself as being the top dog on Carl's yard and she was right – and there were a lot of dogs to top! Lulu was a very good friend to Blueberry, and he was very fond of her. Plus, she always helped him when he was troubled, or when he had a question. Blueberry didn't quite know what he would do without his canine friend.

"But I can do them," Blueberry assured her, not for the first time. "You've seen me do them in the field – and so have other people!"

"Yes, I have, but as I've told you before, you can't run before you can walk, and you can't passage and piaffe before you can do everything

10

else perfectly. If Carl taught you how to do those advanced movements with a rider now, before your muscles are trained, before you can carry yourself correctly and can do all the basic movements perfectly – *perfectly*, mind," she stressed, "you won't do them *properly*. What a lot of people don't realise," Lulu continued, warming to her subject, "is that walking and trotting perfectly can be a lot more difficult than they think and only ignorant people – and horses (and here she gave Blueberry an accusing one-eyed stare, causing his chin to wobble even more) – think they are easy to do. If you don't do them perfectly, You. Will. Mess. Up. Do you want to mess up?"

"No," said Blueberry. He definitely didn't want to mess up. Top dressage horses did not mess up. He wanted to be a top dressage horse. He was *determined* to be a top dressage horse. His ambition, he reminded himself, was to be like The Silver Dancer who stood outside Carl's house. The Silver Dancer, sculpted in metal to dance forever in piaffe, played a big part in Blueberry's inspiration to succeed.

"But I can already walk," he said. "And run. All we do in the school is go around and around – sometimes straight, sometimes in big, sweeping circles, sometimes not at all. Lucy often asks me to stand still and watch while the

11

other horses go around and around, too. I'm not really learning anything."

"Well, that's what you think," Lulu told him. "You just listen to your rider, listen to Carl and, above all kiddo, be patient – which is something Lucy is trying to teach you when you stand still and watch the others. Don't waste that time. Watch and learn from the other horses. You may think you're the next best thing since sliced bread, but even you can't skip the basics."

Blueberry didn't know what sliced bread was, but it didn't sound very impressive. Surely he was better than that – whatever it was. Seeing the doubt in his eyes, Lulu sighed. This little horse, she knew, was highly rated by Carl. She knew, even if Blueberry didn't, that Carl saw something special in him and was watching his progress closely. Carl had put aside the fact that Blueberry was too small to ride himself and was determined to find a special rider who would be able to compete with him in the future. The early work was so important for every horse on the yard, but Lulu understood that part of Blueberry's frustration with his – as he saw it – slow progress was due to his ambition and keenness to do well. He needed to prove his worth to Carl. Lulu understood how Blueberry needed to feel secure and to show everyone, not just Carl, how hard he was prepared to work. Putting her plans aside (she had been looking forward to joining Carl for lunch in the hope that a few tasty morsels might transfer from his plate towards her way), Lulu sat down and began to explain the importance of Blueberry's early work in a way she hoped he would understand.

"You see, kiddo," said Lulu, looking around for inspiration, "it might help to think of your training as being… well, a bit like your stable. How do you think a stable is built?"

Blueberry looked puzzled. It wasn't something he had ever considered. Thinking about it now, he answered slowly, "I suppose people just build it with bricks – I can see how they do it by looking at the walls, one brick on top of the other."

Lulu nodded. "Yes, but before they start building with bricks they have to make sure the ground below is solid and sound. Otherwise, all the bricks would topple over as soon as there was a rainstorm, or the wind blew a bit hard or even if a horse leant on it. Don't worry," she added, seeing Blueberry's look of alarm as he studied the walls of his own stable, "that won't happen because your stable has been built on a solid foundation. The first thing the builders do is dig out a big area where they want the stables to be and put down lots of concrete. This

13

foundation – as it's called – gives a solid base for the stable to be built on. See?"

Blueberry nodded. That made sense. He could imagine that if the bricks were put on the mud, they would just sink.

"A dog can have a lot of fun with unset concrete," Lulu told him, detouring nostalgically from her explanation. "A dog can enjoy quite a reaction from the builders when they come back the next day, having worked hard to get a nice, smooth finish to the surface of the cement, only to be greeted by a row of paw-prints – or even just the occasional single paw-print, nothing too obvious. You probably haven't noticed," Lulu told Blueberry, with pride, "but I made my mark on all these stables when they were being built, left my autograph you might say. I think you've only got one or two prints in the corner, under your manger."

Blueberry looked under his manger. He couldn't see Lulu's paw-prints because of the rubber matting Carl had installed on his stable floor, which meant his stable was springy and comfortable under his hooves, and warm under his bedding when he wanted to lie down. He liked his rubber matting, but all the same he wished he could see Lulu's signature paw prints which were hidden underneath.

"Now," said Lulu, briskly returning to her subject of stable construction, "what do you think would happen if the base of the stable wasn't quite deep enough, or the concrete wasn't quite level, or the people rushed that bit of stable building and put a less than perfect layer of concrete down, or hadn't cleared the earth away properly below it?"

"I would think," said Blueberry, his chin twitching as he thought hard, "that whatever was built on top might suffer and the rest of the stable might not be as strong as it should be."

"Exactly!" cried Lulu, relieved she didn't have to go over it again. "So, why do you think I'm telling you this?" she asked.

Blueberry could almost feel his brain working. "I think," he began, slowly, making sure he got all the words right, "that I need to do all the work Carl is asking me to do now as perfectly as I can so that the rest of my work has a good *foundation* – that's the word, isn't it? That way, the work I do later will be strong, like my stable."

Lulu couldn't have wished for a better answer. She knew her pupil was bright, but that he had understood so quickly what she was trying to tell him impressed her. Not for the first time, she could see why Carl was so excited by this little horse. A good dressage horse needed brains as well as talent.

"Got it in one," Lulu said. "You're concentrating on the foundations now. It will be a while before you progress on to the walls – that will be the next stage of your training, and if you consider how many bricks there are in the walls you will understand how many different things you need to learn – every different movement and lesson is a single brick. Then the windows and door need to go in – another, higher stage – and, finally the roof. When the roof goes on, kiddo, you'll know you've made it as a top dressage horse. The roof," she added, not certain Blueberry had quite got her drift, "is the equivalent to learning passage and piaffe!"

"Thanks, Lulu," said Blueberry, nuzzling his friend. "I'm going to try extra hard to make sure my foundations are the best and strongest they could be. That way, the walls will be super strong, too, ready for the windows and – finally – the roof."

Chapter three

For the horses at Carl's yard, life wasn't just about learning to be dressage horses. Just like people, horses need balance in their lives and as Lulu told Blueberry, 'All work and no play, makes Jack a dull boy!' Blueberry didn't know who Jack was, or what he did to be working all the time (time for Jack to get a new job he decided), but before he could ask Lulu to clarify her words she was off to further her own career – maintaining her status on the yard as top dog, which was especially important since Blueberry had noticed that the dog population at Brook Mill didn't remain static. Apart from the many visitors to Brook Mill – riders, pupils, people who delivered things, professionals who came to see the horses to shoe, massage or treat them – who brought their own dogs who raced around sniffing and making friends with Lulu and Willow (if Lulu was in a good mood, otherwise she took herself off if the visiting dogs were particularly annoying), there were other dogs. These dogs came, stayed a while and then left. Not Lulu and Willow, of course, they were almost part of the furniture, but other dogs didn't seem to be so permanent. The first time Blueberry noticed this was when a medium-sized black dog arrived and began to join everyone on the yard as part of the family. As far as Blueberry could tell, the dog wasn't a specific breed, but she was friendly enough, with an easy wag to her tail, and a very pink tongue like a slice of ham which dangled out of one side of her mouth most of the time, giving her a rather soppy expression.

"Jet?" replied Lulu, when Blueberry asked about the new arrival. "She's okay. Somewhat nervy, but most of them are when they first arrive. Bit clingy – but that's understandable. She won't be here very long, I don't expect."

"Why?" asked Blueberry, not knowing which of his questions to ask first. Should it be about explaining how it was understandable that Jet was clingy, or indeed what clingy meant, or why she was nervy? He had decided the question regarding the length of her stay at Brook Mill would be his first.

"Oh, she'll be snapped up," said Lulu, scratching behind one ear with a hind paw. "Especially with that *'please love me'* look she's so good at."

"Snapped up?" asked Blueberry. Why did Lulu have to speak in riddles? It seemed he never got a straight answer to any of his questions.

"Yup," said Lulu, wondering whether it was time for the staffs' mid-morning break and what type of biscuits they might be having. She hoped it wasn't Rich Tea, as they were quite boring. A Custard Cream or, even better, a Digestive would be perfect, she decided. Thinking it must be about the right time, the little tan-coloured dog wandered off to confirm the biscuit choice, leaving Blueberry to his thoughts.

Blueberry was enjoying his work, but that wasn't all he had to look forward to. Unlike Jack, he and the other horses all had plenty of variety in their lives, which Carl knew was important to keep them happy and far from dull. Between the serious schooling sessions, Blueberry and

19

the other horses all looked forward to going for hacks in the lanes and bridle tracks, and through the woods surrounding Brook Mill Stables. Sometimes, Blueberry hacked out with his friend Orange, and the big chestnut horse's ears twitched as he walked along unknown paths, waiting for something nasty to jump out at him. It never did. At other times Uthopia, the almost black stallion, a year older than Blueberry, came too, but any of the other horses at Carl's might join them. Everyone hacked out – and Blueberry was occasionally ridden by people other than his groom, Lydia, and Carl, riders who were Carl's friends, and very competent riders. It made it all very interesting for the horses and they got used to having different riders on their backs.

Unlike Orange, Blueberry didn't anticipate drama and disaster behind every tree. The little brown horse looked eagerly around him, taking in all the sights, sounds and smells that were unfamiliar, but which he found exciting rather than frightening. To Blueberry, hacking was an adventure whereas to Orange it was more of an ordeal. No two horses are the same but it seemed these two friends were polar opposites.

The best hacks, Blueberry thought, and the ones he looked forward to the most, were the hacks when Carl rode him. He loved being ridden by Lydia, who usually rode him out,

20

and by Lucy, who often schooled him, and all the other riders he had carried had all sat well and still and had given him confidence, but there was something about Carl in his saddle that made Blueberry feel like he was something special. He felt his paces had more quality, his self-carriage (which was the grace, ease and correctness with which he carried himself, and he was working hard on that) became easier, his transitions smoother. Blueberry wished Carl would ride him all the time – he was sure he would become the best dressage horse the world had ever known if that were the case! Of course, what Blueberry didn't realise was that Carl made certain only really good riders were permitted to ride his horses as, in just one hack, an inexperienced or unsympathetic rider could undo the work Carl had taken months to build.

Of course, schooling or hacking didn't take up a whole day. Between work and hacks Blueberry and the other horses were fed, groomed, mucked out, washed off, given time under the warmth of the solarium, received visits from the equine physiotherapist and the masseuse who stroked and pummelled their muscles to make them feel great – and even an equine back specialist to ensure their backs were healthy and strong. Blueberry enjoyed looking out over his top door from his stable in the corner of the yard, watching all the comings and goings and stretching out his nose to the passing grooms and riders in order to grab a pat and a quick word. There was always something to see, always someone to talk to and always lots to learn.

Between all this activity, every horse at Brook Mill Stables enjoyed time off in the field – and Blueberry was no exception. 'Horses need time to be horses,' Carl said, and even when it was raining, and the mud oozed around the horses' hooves, splashing their legs and bellies as they galloped around, the horses were all turned out in a field each day to enjoy their down-time. Some excitable horses even lived out in the larger fields all the time. In the winter the horses wore neck coverings and hoods attached to their waterproof rugs, so that when they rolled the mud didn't seep into their manes, tangling them. Roll they usually did, grunting loudly as they sank down, their legs waving in the air as they turned onto their backs, rolling from one side to the other before hauling themselves up again and galloping off, bucking and leaping, to see which of them could throw clods of earth from their hooves the highest, the farthest. If they managed to shower the grooms, who stood at the gate watching them, with mud that was even more fun. Whenever he rolled, Blueberry always made it a point of honour to ensure he rolled right over from one side to the other – not all the horses could manage it. Those who couldn't often had to get up and sink down again to roll on their other side, but Blueberry never had to do that. He considered it a matter of honour to roll right over every time!

Going out in the field was even better in the summer when the sun shone and Blueberry could feel the warmth of it on his back. The grass felt good as he rolled, scratching all his itchy parts. It was nature's massage, helping his overall sense of well-being. The only time being out wasn't so good was in the height of summer, when the flies came out and settled on the horses' faces and flanks, causing them to shake their heads and swish their tails. On these days, rather than keep the horses in their stables, they were turned out early in the morning, and Lydia sprayed Blueberry with a special fly repellent (Orange had to have the repellent sprayed onto a cloth and wiped over his body as he panicked at the *tsss-tsss* sound of the spray). One very hot day, Lydia fitted the horses with special lightweight rugs with a zig-zag stripe design, transforming them both into make-believe zebras.

"There you go!" Lydia announced, standing back and observing her charges' new look.

"These stripes will confuse the flies – it's one of the reasons zebras have stripes. There are more flies in Africa than there are here!"

Blueberry didn't know where Africa was and he'd never seen a zebra, but he could see the stripes on Orange's rug and wondered if he looked just as comical. Lulu, on her way to a sniff-a-thon in the adjoining field, had something to say about it – namely that Blueberry looked ridiculous. He didn't mind – he hated the flies and anything that discouraged them was fine with him. If it was a choice between staying in his stable and looking cool, or wearing the zebra rug and being able to eat grass, he'd choose his fancy dress any day because Blueberry loved eating! As well as all the fun he had rolling and galloping around with his friends, Blueberry ate as much grass as he could cram in during his turn-out time. Lulu once asked him whether he wished he'd been born a cow, which had thrown Blueberry into a spin. Why would he want to be a cow? Cows didn't compete in dressage, did they? You didn't see cows at Carl's yard having their saddles fitted, perfecting their canter down the centre line in the school, lining up to have new shoes fitted to their cloven hooves? The idea was ludicrous! There was quite a lot of confused-chin-wobbling until Lulu explained that cows had four stomachs and Blueberry realised his friend had cracked a joke. It was a joke at his expense, he realised, but it was quite funny. He wouldn't want to be a cow, the little brown horse decided, but he thought it might be fun to have all those stomachs!

Chapter four

I t was only a week or so later, around lunchtime (Blueberry was always looking out over his stable door around lunchtime to remind Lydia that he was a growing horse and needed his meals on time), when Blueberry realised he hadn't seen the new black dog, Jet, around the yard for at least a couple of days.

"Have you seen Jet?" Blueberry asked Orange, who was also looking out into the yard and listening for the familiar sound of the feed buckets. They both spotted Lydia going into the feed room and Jet was forgotten for a few seconds until Lydia returned to the yard empty-handed, and walked briskly over to the tack room.

"Who?" asked Orange, in a distracted yet impatient way. Where *was* lunch?

"Jet," said Blueberry. "That nice black dog. Bit ditzy."

"Oh yes, I know the one. I saw her get into someone's car – that young girl who came for a couple of lessons. I didn't see her get out again and the girl and her father drove off. I suppose Jet went with them."

"What?" cried Blueberry. "You mean they just took her?" He could hardly believe his ears, which swivelled wildly in panic. He had to talk to Lulu about this. What if Carl didn't know? What if the girl and her father had taken something else? Whinnying loudly, Blueberry was glad to see the sight of a short-legged, tan-coloured, one-eyed dog trotting into the yard, wondering what all the fuss was about.

"It's Jet," Blueberry panted, all thought of lunch forgotten. "She's been stolen by that girl who came for lessons. Orange saw her get in their car!"

Lulu stared at him and sighed. Blueberry didn't know how a small dog could put so much disdain in a look from one eye, but Lulu managed it. Actually, he thought, she completely smashed it.

27

"I did tell you, didn't I, that Jet would soon be leaving. Don't you remember?"

Blueberry did. He just hadn't remembered until Lulu reminded him just now.

"And you remember what I told you about…" Lulu looked around to see whether the big mastiff-cross dog was around before lowering her voice so only Blueberry could hear her. "… about Willow, and how he came to live here, with Carl?"

"Yes," nodded Blueberry, "of course." Poor Willow had been found in London, tied to park railings, left there by his previous owners. *Thrown away*, was how Lulu had put it. Luckily, the big gentle dog had been taken to the dogs' home where Carl had found him later and brought him to his forever home at Brook Mill. But even though Willow had never forgotten Carl's kindness, and loved him more than life itself, he could also never forget his traumatic experience and that sometimes made him sad.

"Well, Jet had a similar history," explained Lulu. "She too was unwanted and Carl brought her here. But he can't keep all the dogs he rescues, you know. This is, in case you've forgotten, a dressage yard, not a dogs' home. So, when people come to have lessons, or work for Carl or even just visit, he introduces them to the new arrivals. And hey presto what do you

28

know, the visitors fall in love with the dogs and wonder if Carl could possibly part with them, promising a forever home with them. The dog gets a brilliant, horsey home and the new owner is thrilled to think they have a dog that used to belong to Carl. It's a perfect win-win scenario, kiddo."

Blueberry thought this over. It seemed to be a brilliant idea, an idea which worked. But then…

"He doesn't do it with horses, does he?" Blueberry asked, holding his breath until Lulu answered.

"No, stop worrying," she replied. "Here's lunch, if I'm not very much mistaken."

Blueberry had been so captivated by hearing about Carl's patented dog re-homing scheme he hadn't noticed Lydia arriving with a bucket of his favourite feed. Once the feed was in his manger, however, all thoughts of Jet disappeared as he gave his full attention to lunch.

Chapter five

Sometimes, Blueberry's enthusiasm for his lessons hindered rather than helped him. He had boundless energy, his canter strides were huge, and whenever Carl, Lucy or any of the other riders asked him for canter they were all impressed by the power they could feel coming through from the hindquarters – the engine – of the little brown horse. Lucy laughed when she told Carl she felt as though she might be pinged out of the saddle and over Blueberry's neat ears! The horse was small, but he was full of energy and able to propel himself forward like a bouncy rocket whenever he was asked. It was obvious he enjoyed showing off his ability, but he hadn't yet realised that dressage horses needed not only to be powerful, but had to be able to switch off and chill when asked.

"Okay Lucy," Carl would call after ten minutes of work, "Ask Blueberry to walk on a long rein."

And Lucy would sit up and slow Blueberry to a walk and let out his reins to encourage him to stretch his neck down while keeping a soft contact on the bit. Blueberry didn't know it, but this was a required movement in dressage tests. It demonstrated that the horse was calm enough to take a short break from his work and stretch his neck, rather than be so wound up and stressed that the rider feared loosening the reins in case the horse just fizzed and jogged in excitement. Blueberry didn't fizz and jog – his lessons were never stressful enough to cause him to get over-excited – but he was just so keen to be the perfect equine student he was always on the alert for the next instruction, the next lesson. Blueberry didn't realise that walking on a long rein *was* the next lesson! This meant that rather than relaxing and stretching his neck down to keep the contact, he often lifted his head and looked around him, looking at what the other horses were doing, or glancing back at Lucy to try to guess what she might want him to do next. He could feel she had some rein contact – so what on earth did she want him to do?

The little brown horse was already familiar with his rider letting out the reins altogether and holding them at the buckle when it was a rest period or time to stop working. Blueberry was having difficulty in distinguishing between his free walk on a *long* rein – where the rider maintains a contact on the reins for a stretch between movements – and walking on a *loose* rein – where the rider has no contact and the horse drops his head and walks how he likes, taking a mini-break from, or winding down after, schooling.

"Oh dear," sighed Carl, shaking his head. The little brown horse didn't look terribly relaxed on a long rein. He looked eager to get on with his lessons, keen to trot and canter some more. His keenness could easily be mistaken for being uptight in a dressage test. "We need to work on that!" Carl told Lucy, as she looked across at Carl and shrugged her shoulders.

It is very easy for a rider to transmit any tension in their own bodies to the horse they are

32

riding. Lucy knew this and always made sure she breathed out into her stomach, rather than her chest, as she asked Blueberry to walk on a long rein so that she wasn't holding her breath, wobbling as she breathed or sitting in a tense way, anticipating that Blueberry would lift his head. Carl asked her to sit tall and drop all her weight down through the saddle, keeping her limbs loose, singing a song in her head to make certain Blueberry had no tension to pick up from his rider. Still he lifted his head to look around him – when the dressage judges would be looking to see him drop his head and stretch his neck, and mark him for it as a movement.

Carl thought hard. Blueberry wasn't doing anything wrong; he just didn't understand what was required from him. How could he tell him what he wanted? What motivated the little brown horse? He couldn't push his head down! Blueberry's motivation was to see what was going on, to take in everything around him rather than drop his head and stretch his neck. Carl even noticed that Blueberry liked to sneak a peek of himself as he walked past the mirrors positioned around the arena. It wasn't so much that the horse was vain, he was just interested in everything going on and it fascinated him to see himself carrying Lucy, or another rider. It made him feel very grown-up! But that didn't help with the stretching-his-neck business. What, thought Carl, would encourage him to do that?

Carl looked around him. The outdoor arena had open sides, without fences. This was so that the horses – and riders – didn't get used to the false security a fence could offer them. Riding next to a fence could encourage riders to ride only one side of their horses, the side *away* from the fence. A fence helped to keep a horse straight – but Carl wanted the riders to ride both sides of their horses! Whether the arena had a fence or not had no bearing on this hiccup of Blueberry's, Carl thought, but without one it meant they could easily hop off the surface and on to the grass…

"Take up your reins, Lucy," Carl instructed, "and follow me."

Carl stepped off the arena surface, on to the grass and Lucy steered Blueberry to follow him. Listening to Carl's instructions, Lucy asked Blueberry to walk and trot around an imaginary arena on the grass. The grass was quite long – it hadn't been mowed for a few days and it had grown wildly following some enthusiastic downpours during the last few nights. Blueberry, greedy as always for a snack or two, eyed it up as he trotted around. That grass looked good! Pity he was being ridden and not turned out in the field, he thought. But then, he did always sneak a bite or two when he was hacking…

34

"Now ask for walk," Carl called to Lucy, "a walk on a long rein." If he was right, Blueberry's greed would help their cause.

Blueberry felt the reins loosening. Instead of looking around him, he looked down at all the luscious grass. Yum, he thought. The reins were so long he could almost… if nobody minded… he wondered whether they would…

He stretched down and nibbled the tops of the grass as he walked along. Lucy rubbed his neck, feeling him stretch, the contact on the bit still there.

"Good boy, Blueberry," she cooed at him, "*streeeetch*." She looked over at Carl and smiled.

Carl grinned back. He had been right; Blueberry's love of his stomach had shown him the way to stretch down when asked. A few more lessons out here on the grass should do the trick and teach the little brown horse what was required. Carl shook his head and smiled to himself. Blueberry was certainly one smart horse – it was sometimes difficult to stay one step ahead of him!

Chapter six

One day, a horsebox rolled into the yard and a striking, bright bay horse with a white blaze running down its face and over its nostrils was led down the ramp and into one of the spare boxes on the outside yard. Blueberry looked over his stable door and through the arch with interest. Was this a horse in for schooling or had its owner come for lessons, he wondered. He thought Lulu might know.

Lulu did know.

"The bright bay?" she said, when Blueberry asked her. "Carl has him in to school on and then find a good home for him."

Blueberry gulped. Lulu reassured him. "Carl isn't going to do that with you, silly. You know he's made up his mind you're staying. Stop worrying."

Blueberry felt better even though, sometimes, Blueberry worried that Carl might change his mind again. After all, the little brown horse was still small compared to the other horses on the yard. There was nothing Blueberry could do to change that, and it had been his size which had worried Carl before. He had no idea of Carl's plans to find a rider worthy of him.

"What's his name and how long do you think he'll stay?" asked Blueberry, wondering whether he'd get the chance to talk to the new horse. He liked making new friends.

"Regency, and I don't know," said Lulu, answering both questions as best she could.

Blueberry got his chance to meet Regency the next day when the bay was turned out in the field where he and Orange were grazing. Excited and eager to make friends, both horses raced over to the gate to say hello. But making friends was the last thing on the bay's mind.

"Hi," said Blueberry, grass still hanging out of his mouth. "I'm Blueberry and this is Orange. You're Regency, aren't you?"

Regency stood by the gate, the whites of his eyes showing, his hind legs quivering. For a moment, Blueberry wondered whether he was going to try to bite him, but he had misread the signs.

"What is this place?" Regency whispered, standing very still.

"You're at Carl's," Blueberry told him. "You're lucky, Brook Mill is a fabulous place and Carl is a brilliant dressage rider and teacher. If he's schooling you, you're in luck!"

"No, this place, this place where we are now," said Regency, breathlessly.

"It's the field, of course," said Orange, snorting. "Don't you know what a field is?"

"No," Regency replied. "And I don't like it. It's big. It's too big, too, too big."

Blueberry was puzzled. To him, the bigger the field, the better. More grass to eat, more room in which to gallop, more places to roll. How could a field be too big?

"You should see the far field," said Orange. "This one is a paddock by comparison, the far field is huge, with lots more grass – oh and you can see the hills in the distance. It's that's big!"

Regency closed his eyes at the thought of

seeing hills in the distance. Blueberry could see that he was in real distress and it puzzled him. He couldn't imagine what might be wrong.

"Haven't you ever been in a field before?" asked Orange. Here was a horse that seemed more nervous that he, which made a change. It made Orange feel quite brave. He liked that feeling – even though he didn't think it would last.

"Never," Regency told him. He still hadn't moved.

"Why don't you come away from the gate?" asked Blueberry, kindly. "Look, there's lots of grass here for you to eat. You like grass, don't you?"

"Of course," replied Regency. "But I've only ever eaten it when I've been led out of my stable on the lead rein. I would like to go back to my stable. I don't like this, this… *field*." Turning around just enough to face the gate Regency lifted his head and neighed loudly, calling to be taken back in, the panic obvious in his neigh.

"Don't be hasty," said Orange, his ears flicking back and forth at the sound of Regency's insistent neighing.

"Won't you even try it out?" asked Blueberry. "After all, we're here, it's not like you're on your own. We're here, nothing bad will happen to you."

"Excuse me," said Regency, walking stiff-legged along the fence past Blueberry and Orange, before turning and walking back – again parallel and as close to the fence as possible – to the same distance the other side of the gate, neighing all the time.

It wasn't long before Lydia appeared, looking worried.

"Thank goodness," sighed Regency dramatically, leaning over the gate. "Somebody has come for me."

"They said you hadn't been turned out much," Lydia murmured, her hands on her hips, "but it looks to me as though you've never been turned out at all. You're getting yourself in a state, aren't you," she added, noticing damp patches of sweat on Regency's neck. "Come on, silly, no use leaving you out here. I'm sure Carl will have an idea about this. If only people would turn their horses out instead of keeping them cooped up in a stable like a rabbit!" Lydia muttered crossly, clipping the lead rope to Regency's headcollar and leading him out of the gate and back to the yard. Regency trotted along beside her in relief, tugging at the lead rope in his hurry to get back to the familiar safety of his stable's four walls.

Blueberry and Orange didn't know quite what to make of it all.

"That's sad," sighed Blueberry, eventually.

Orange thought so too. "I can't imagine life without coming out in the field," he said, staring into the distance, trying very hard to imagine it anyway.

Blueberry shuddered. Never being turned out in the field was totally unimaginable to him. "We have to think of a way to help Regency," he said. "All horses should enjoy time out in the field. We just have to think of something."

Orange agreed, although he couldn't for the life of him imagine what that something might be.

41

Chapter seven

Blueberry continued to enjoy his lessons, trying really hard to please, and he learned more and more. He started to understand just how far he had come and could tell the difference between how he moved under his rider now, to how he had moved before his lessons. He realised that he wasn't just walking, trotting and cantering around. His paces were more rhythmic, steady and consistent. He now sprang from his hind legs with more control, propelling himself along with grace as well as strength, and he was beginning to make his transitions exactly when asked, with no middle, muddling, in-between pace, but springing from walk to trot, and trot to canter with quality and energy. Lulu had been right, Blueberry realised, even just walking and trotting could be more difficult than he had thought and he tried his hardest to make sure his paces were as perfect as they could be, rather than just any-old-how. He was starting to appreciate just how far he had progressed in a short space of time. How could he ever have thought that he wasn't learning anything?

The horses weren't always ridden in the same place: sometimes they were ridden in the outdoor arena, other times in the field where there were white boards laid out in a rectangle with letters placed around them (and whenever he was being ridden within the white boards Carl and Lucy were very serious and extra precise – Blueberry had to do everything exactly as he was asked, where he was asked to do it, even though his time there was much shorter than anywhere else, and the movements asked of him quite simple), or in the indoor arena where people sometimes sat and watched, with its glaring electric lights in the roof so the horses could be ridden even when it was dark outside, or if it were raining.

Blueberry's friend Orange wasn't very keen on working inside. The big chestnut was much more nervous than the little brown horse, and Carl and his staff were sympathetic knowing that all horses – just like people – were different and had their own quirks. Whenever they worked together in the indoor school Blueberry found it difficult to understand the way Orange was easily distracted. Sometimes the wind rattled the walls. Sometimes the doves would fly from their perches on the lights; the sudden, overhead movement startling Orange. Sometimes, the dogs would run along the outside of the open wall playing and making a noise. The horses could hear them, but they couldn't see the dogs, which was very off-putting for Orange when he was trying to concentrate on walking in a perfectly straight line, or when he was cantering around the outside track. But as his lessons inside increased Orange gradually realised that nothing was going to harm him, and he began to relax and concentrate. Even so, he was always on the lookout for anything out of the ordinary which might spell danger.

Blueberry, on the other hand, didn't mind where he worked. He found he became so engrossed in what his rider was asking him, and listening so hard to Carl so he could get the most out of every session, he hardly had any room left in his brain for distractions. When something unexpected did happen – one of the cats leapt into the arena under his nose one windy day, chasing a leaf which resembled a

44

mouse – Blueberry made sure he tried very hard to continue in trot, rather than shy or stop. Carl seemed very pleased with his efforts. That there were lots of distractions at Brook Mill was intentional as Carl knew that horses needed to practise their concentration. If it was easily lost then they would find competing in different places, with different noises, sounds and smells very difficult. If they could work well despite all the interruptions, they would find performing at competitions much easier.

Blueberry was learning much more than he could ever have imagined.

Chapter eight

Blueberry hadn't yet had a chance to make friends with Brook Mill's stable cats, Bonnie and Clyde – mainly because they were not always around. Bonnie was a pretty tortoiseshell colour, a mixture of red and browns with the occasional fleck of white, while Clyde was pale ginger. Blueberry could tell that Lydia thought a lot of them both, she was always leaning down to stroke them when they were on the yard, or talking to them when she sometimes sat on one of the seats on a warm day and ate her lunch. Bonnie in particular seemed to like Lydia very much when she had sandwiches. Blueberry couldn't help noticing that the cats had a particularly superior way with them as they sat on a stable door, a roof or on top of the hay bales in the barn. It always seemed to him that whenever either of them looked his way their whole demeanour said that they were in possession of an important secret which he would – and could – never understand.

Blueberry wished he could get to know them better. He felt sure that if Lydia liked them, they weren't as superior in manner as they appeared. He made the mistake of thinking Lulu shared Lydia's feelings for the cats. Lulu put him straight as soon as he asked about them, advising him not to give the cats the satisfaction of showing any curiosity about them *whatsoever*. She particularly stressed the last word.

"Don't encourage them," she said, narrowing her one good eye which suggested she had little respect for either Bonnie or Clyde. "I wouldn't give them the time of day."

"I've seen Willow chasing them," Blueberry told her, wondering why the cats would want to know the time. He knew he wouldn't be able to

tell them, even if they asked him. He had seen
Willow bounding after the cats several times.
Whenever he caught sight of either Bonnie or
Clyde the big dog went from nought-to-sixty in
three bounds, growling fiercely. But however
fast he moved, the cats always moved faster
and usually leapt up a tree or a fence out of
reach. And Blueberry noticed that, even though
they managed to move at lightning speed,
they managed to maintain their feline-superior
manner. It was most strange – and, he couldn't
help thinking – rather impressive.

"The thing is," said Lulu, looking around
to make sure neither Bonnie nor Clyde were in
earshot, "a person – and by that," she explained,
"I mean a *canine* person – can waste a lot of
energy chasing things which are never, ever
going to be caught. All it does is wear out the
chaser, and amuses the chasee. The trouble
with cats is that, not only are they fast but they
can also leap and climb so they get themselves
up high and out of reach. Believe me, there is
nothing more humiliating than being looked
down from on high by a smug cat. Fair does a
dog's head in, that does. I've told Willow this
over and over again, but does he listen?"

Blueberry guessed that the answer to
that question was no. Then he remembered
something else. "Willow sometimes chases the

48

guinea-fowl, too. Carl is always telling him not to." The guinea-fowl were wild, but they often hung around the field and outdoor arena, bobbing along in a line, nervously glancing around and giving each other the courage to keep going. They made a colourful addition to the yard menagerie.

"That's right," agreed Lulu, nodding. "The guinea-fowl would be easier to catch and Willow knows it. Carl forbids it absolutely. He likes the guinea-fowl around. The trouble is, Willow gets very excited at the thought of chasing something – he has no self-control and is a martyr to his instincts. I've even seen him eying up the hens when he thinks no-one is looking. And," Lulu agreed, tilting her head and nodding in a knowing way, "a chase can be good fun. I myself intend to catch that squirrel that hangs around one day – I'll catch it off-guard eventually when Carl isn't around. But the guinea-fowl are part of the family at Brook Mill, and Willow should respect that."

Blueberry didn't really understand why Willow wanted to chase the guinea-fowl or the hens, but he did sort of get why he wanted to chase Bonnie and Clyde if they looked at Willow with that same superior look they used when they surveyed him. He doubted the squirrel was in any danger, though, he'd seen how fast it shot

49

up trees, and he knew Lulu couldn't reach even the lowest branches. The squirrel, Blueberry concluded, was safe enough.

"What do the cats do?" Blueberry asked Lulu, who was starting to get bored with all the cat chat.

"Do?" she replied. "Do? The cats? Good question! They don't *do* anything. They're supposed to keep the mouse population down but they're so well fed they just sit about all day and stare in that green-eyed way of theirs, or sleep. *Do* isn't in a cat's vocabulary. What they *do* is take up space! You're better off asking what they *don't*! I've a huge list of *don'ts* that apply to cats! And I'm a better mouser than either of them – no, make that *both* of them!"

And that, Blueberry realised as he watched Lulu walking away from his stable and out of the yard, was the end of his lesson about cats, according to Lulu. The way Lulu was walking, stiff-legged with her short tail in the air, suggested that the subject was well and truly closed and he was in no doubt that when it came to Bonnie and Clyde, Lulu wasn't a fan. Blueberry wondered whether Lulu would mind if he made an attempt to get to know Bonnie and Clyde better. It seemed to him, if Willow and Lulu's behaviour was anything to go by, that dogs and cats were never going to be the best of friends but humans and

50

cats enjoyed a very different relationship. Maybe horses and cats could get along and it wouldn't hurt to try, he decided. It was strange how Lulu's opinion differed so widely from Lydia's when it came to felines. Blueberry decided that he would have to make up his own mind about Bonnie and Clyde, rather than depend on someone else's judgement.

A chance for Blueberry to put his plan into action occurred only a few days later. It was lunchtime, all the horses had been fed and the stable staff were all enjoying their own lunch when Blueberry, still licking his lips to get to the last of his feed off his muzzle, looked out over his stable door to see Clyde sitting under one of the trees in the yard, washing himself. Blueberry had noticed that both cats did that a lot. It seemed that whereas Lydia spent a lot of time grooming Blueberry with brushes and wiping him over to make him look spick-and-span, nobody groomed the cats but themselves. Blueberry watched, impressed. He knew that even if he wanted to, or had to, he couldn't possibly reach all the bits of himself with his own tongue to make himself tidy, but Clyde could bend himself into all sorts of positions to reach all those places Blueberry decided he'd actually rather not reach. Not for the first time he was pretty glad he wasn't a cat.

51

"How do you do that?" asked Blueberry, unable to stay quiet any longer. Clyde's head had disappeared and one hind leg stuck up like a flag pole. Clyde came up for air and looked across at Blueberry.

"Well, since you ask I, like all cats, possess a flexible backbone," Clyde explained. "Didn't you know?"

"No," said Blueberry. "I don't know anything about cats – except that you and the dogs don't seem to get on."

Clyde's green eyes glinted. "Dogs are inferior beings to cats," he said. "And they waste energy. You never see a cat wasting energy like a dog."

So, thought Blueberry, it seemed that this dog-cat-dislike thing was mutual. Neither species liked the other. Clyde even agreed, sort of, with Lulu when it came to energy and the wasting of it. He decided neither to point that out, nor to take sides.

"I've noticed you can climb and jump higher than dogs," said Blueberry, thinking flattery might get Clyde on-side. He was right.

"You're observant," said Clyde, ending his wash. "Cats have plenty of fascinating attributes which are not always appreciated. We have nine lives, for example, and we always – but always – land on our feet, no matter how high we fall from, or the position our bodies started from.

When it comes to it, we are totally superior to dogs in every way, which, of course, annoys them even more."

Blueberry thought hard. Nine lives? Surely that couldn't be right. He didn't want to go into that right now; he didn't want to sound stupid for not understanding what Clyde meant. As for cats landing on their feet, that sounded like a useful skill to have. He said so.

"Yes, well, it comes in handy," agreed Clyde. "It's necessary for a species which climbs a lot."

Blueberry could appreciate that. So much for their differences, he thought, but did they share any common ground? "Do cats do dressage?" he asked.

Clyde gave him a look. "Certainly not," he said, "we are above such things. But you all seem to like it, and it looks very elegant. I quite enjoy watching all the horses here perform their graceful movements. Of course, cats have natural grace. I'm not saying that we *wouldn't* be able to perform dressage – we'd be excellent at it – but it's more that cats are their own masters. We only do what we want to do. And that, to be honest, consists mainly of sitting in the sun, cleaning ourselves, eating – of course – and sitting on laps and being stroked. It's a great life, being a cat. You should try it. Only, of course, you'd be hard pushed to find a lap big enough to sit on."

There was no arguing with that, thought Blueberry. He was going to ask another question but it seemed that Clyde had somewhere to be and he watched him saunter silently across the yard, his tail waving like a stalk of grass in the wind. He didn't seem so bad, Blueberry thought, quite friendly, in a sort of self-contained, not over-enthusiastic way. Even so, he decided, maybe it would be better not to tell Lulu about his new friend.

Chapter nine

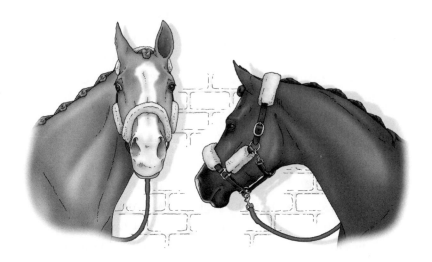

"Come on Blueberry," said Lydia, fastening Blueberry's headcollar and leading him to the washing boxes. "Let's get you polished up for your first party!"

Blueberry was used to being washed. The warm water felt good – but usually this happened after a work session, or even when he came in from the field covered in mud or dust, not first thing in the morning. And what did Lydia mean by his first party? Blueberry looked around for Lulu, she always knew everything and could answer his questions but right now, annoyingly, she had other things to do. It could be she was on one of her epic sniff-a-thons around the stables and fields, or sitting with Carl while he was teaching, or even watching the special hole in the barn which sometimes a rat or a mouse might use as a doorway – before wishing it hadn't.

Once Blueberry's coat was clean and wet he stood under the solarium to dry off and Lydia fussed around him brushing his mane and tail and making sure his four white legs gleamed like snow. She even polished his hooves and rubbed a towel around his face and mouth to make sure he was as clean as possible. Lydia always gave him a thorough grooming and kept him looking spick-and-span, but this morning she was even more exacting and Blueberry felt as though he was glowing by the time she declared him done and threw a lightweight rug over his quarters to keep the dust off. It wasn't his usual rug, but one with Carl's name on either side. Blueberry had seen other horses on the yard wearing similar rugs and he suddenly felt the first stirring of excitement in his stomach. There was something about these rugs that was special – what was it?

And then Lydia did something she had never done before; climbing up onto a stool near his front off-side hoof she divided the little brown horse's mane into even bunches with bands. Blueberry could feel them on his neck. Then, starting behind his ears, he felt her divide the first bunch still further and start doing something weird with the hair. She rolled it under itself and then, out of the corner of his eye, Blueberry saw her lift a needle and thread from her jumper, and stick the needle in his mane. Blueberry froze – but he didn't feel anything. No pricking of a needle, no blood running down his neck. Phew! He'd been worried for a moment – he knew all about needles from visits from the vet. It seemed a very strange thing for Lydia to do, but eventually she snipped the remaining thread with some scissors and began the same treatment with the next bunch of hair – and that didn't hurt either. Blueberry shook his head – and heard a protesting shout from Lydia who, she told him, now needed to start that plait again.

Plaits! Blueberry had seen plaits on the other horses. Their manes had been neatly plaited and rolled up to sit at the top of their crests, showing off their necks. The only time they'd been plaited had been when they had gone somewhere. And then he remembered that the plaited horses had also worn the rugs with Carl's name on the sides. Blueberry felt excitement growing within him. If his mane was being plaited, then could it be possible that …?

Next to him, Orange was receiving the same treatment from one of the other grooms. "I do hope we're not off to a competition," said Orange, rolling his eyes. "I'm so not ready for that!"

Blueberry's hopes were confirmed. If they were being plaited, then surely they *must* be going to a competition. Why hadn't he realised before? Trying to keep his excitement under control, he looked over through the arch in the stable yard. Sure enough the horsebox was there, the ramp lowered, haynets already tied inside, clean bedding awaiting them.

"Please try to keep still, Blueberry," wailed Lydia, leaning over from her stool and trying to keep the plait she was half-way through intact. Blueberry stood like a rock so she could finish his mane. He didn't want to do anything that might stop him going to his first competition! After Lydia had moved around to the front of him and deftly plaited his forelock, she gave the little brown horse a treat for being so good, fastened his rug and disappeared to load his and Orange's tack into a trunk and onto the horsebox.

Blueberry arched his neck, which felt weird. He was used to feeling his mane on his neck and his forelock on his forehead but now he felt quite stripped. He felt – he strained to find the right word and wished Lulu was there to help him, – he felt *streamlined*, he decided. Then he realised Lydia had missed the last two bunches by his withers where his rug rested. He wouldn't worry about that, he thought. Lydia must know what she was doing.

After a short time Lydia was back, fastening the rope on his headcollar and leading an eager Blueberry out of his stable and up the ramp of the horsebox before returning for Orange, who was also plaited and looking not only very smart, but also extremely anxious. Blueberry noticed his friend's final two mane bunches were also left unplaited, which reassured him that it was not a mistake.

"You are a worrier," said Lydia, patting the chestnut's gleaming neck, "and I don't know why – no one has ever asked you to do anything you're not capable of. I wish you'd relax and chill out a bit, like Blueberry."

Orange just snorted and looked back at the yard as though he wished he was still on it.

"This is going to be fun!" Blueberry told him, his friend firmly disagreeing with him. Blueberry was disappointed he still hadn't been able to talk to Lulu – he was sure she would want to wish him good luck. Just before the ramp was raised Blueberry spied Willow wandering about, looking for something he might be able to chase in a subtle way while Carl wasn't around.

"Hey, Willow!" called Blueberry. "Tell Lulu I'm off to a competition!"

The ramp was put up before Blueberry could hear Willow's reply and it wasn't long before the horsebox rumbled down the drive and on its way.

Chapter ten

When the horsebox reached its destination and Lydia led Blueberry down the ramp, the little brown horse couldn't help feeling disappointed. He didn't know what a competition was going to look like, but this place they had come to looked just like someone else's stable yard – and there didn't seem to be many people there to watch his dressage debut. Blueberry had it in his head that competitions were where lots of people watched the dressage tests – that was what Uthopia had told him. Perhaps, thought Blueberry, this was such a tiny, unimportant competition that nobody wanted to come and watch. Or maybe, he thought, his hopes rising, he and Orange had arrived so early the crowds were still on their way.

He was wrong on both counts.

Folding back his rug, Lydia quickly plaited Blueberry's final two bunches which might otherwise have been rubbed by the rug on the journey, tacked him up and gave his hooves another polish. "No need to worry about anything," she whispered in his ear, "just be your usual, gorgeous, self!"

"Blueberry looks amazing Lydia. Are we ready?" said another voice, and Blueberry turned to see Lucy, smartly dressed in a black jacket, a white stock around her neck, with white breeches and long black boots so polished they glinted in the sun.

It hadn't occurred to Blueberry that the riders would wear something different for competitions, but seeing Lucy in all her finery he realised how special she looked, and how smart they were both going to appear. Dressage is an elegant sport and the overall look of horse and rider is part of the whole package. Of course, it doesn't make any difference to how the horse moves, nor can it improve the partnership's performance, but it enhances the whole look and gives a polished edge. Looking at Lucy and his own dazzling white legs and polished hooves, Blueberry felt very proud and determined to do his best. You could say it lifted his spirits and encouraged him to rise to the occasion.

With Lucy on board, the pair made their way to the outdoor arena – which was like the one at Brook Mill – and warmed up. Blueberry didn't realise this was what they were doing; to him they were just riding around like they did at home, walking, trotting, cantering, and avoiding the few other horses who were doing the same. It was a big arena but there were some jumps set up inside, which had to be avoided. Riding around with the other horses was also distracting but, gradually, Blueberry grew accustomed to all the new sights, sounds and smells and began to listen more to his rider.

Once she felt Blueberry had loosened up from the journey, and was moving fluently and freely, Lucy asked the little brown horse to move more accurately and perform some transitions and halts. Blueberry tried hard to do what Lucy asked him as well as he could – but it was more difficult here, thinking he was at a competition, than at home. He could see Orange, who was quite jumpy and taking longer to settle than he was. Orange was obviously anxious about the whole set up. He didn't embrace new experiences like Blueberry did. Working around horses he didn't know was difficult. As Blueberry trotted past some he could feel they were unsure of him, too, and therefore wary of him. Others seemed more friendly, and he wished he could stop for a chat and exchange stories about how they had reached this point in their careers but, of course, he couldn't. He had to listen to Lucy and concentrate on his work. Blueberry hadn't realised it would be this difficult.

Lucy knew Blueberry would be experiencing all these feelings, which was why warming up well was so important. You couldn't expect a horse, particularly a young, inexperienced horse, to jump off the horsebox and go straight into a test! Dressage horses are athletes and need the same preparation as any other. Carl had chosen this outing with care – it was to be a good and undemanding introduction for Blueberry and Orange to experience a competitive atmosphere and he would be taking great interest in the two horses. Unbeknown to Blueberry and Orange, Carl was watching from a distance and already he could see the difference between how his two young hopefuls were coping with the day.

Gradually, Lucy felt Blueberry relax beneath her. She could feel he was excited and bouncy,

64

but he was listening to her so she nodded to Carl, hidden from view. Blueberry felt himself relax, too. This was fun! All these horses, Lucy on board giving him confidence – it was exciting. He couldn't wait to perform and he wondered what he would need to do, what Lucy would ask of him, and how he would do against the others. Wouldn't it be amazing if he won? Seeing all the others he could tell that some horses were far more highly trained than he was, so he was a bit disappointed – of course he wouldn't win against such experienced competition. It didn't seem quite fair, it was obvious some had been to lots of competitions before, but he trusted Carl knew what he was doing. Thinking back to Lulu's talk about his stable, and likening it to a horse's training, Blueberry could see that, whereas he was still on his first row of bricks, some of the other horses' stables had most of the walls built and even some of the windows fitted! He was still a bit worried that there were not many people about to watch. As far as he could see, there were only the grooms and trainers of the other horses around.

"Right Blueberry," Lucy said, leaning forward in the saddle to pat his neck, "let's show them what you're made of!" Blueberry's chin wobbled. That sounded sinister, and he wasn't sure he wanted the judges to know what he was made of, but he hoped Lucy didn't really mean that. Sometimes, Blueberry acknowledged, Carl and Lucy spoke in the same, strange way Lulu did. He was getting used to that.

Chapter eleven

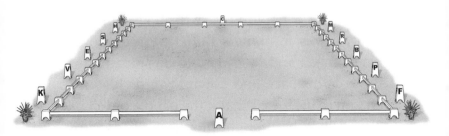

They headed out of the outdoor arena, along a pathway to a huge indoor school where another horse, a large liver chestnut with a red-faced girl on board, was coming out in a relaxed manner, its head low on a long rein. Lucy steered Blueberry through the doors and into the school. Light flooded in through skylights and Blueberry could see white boards like the ones they had a home in the field, and a row of people in the stands beside him, all eyes on him. His audience!

True, it wasn't the huge crowds he had dreamed of, only a couple of dozen people, but it was a start. He and Lucy walked around and Blueberry looked left and right, taking it all in. It was certainly a smart place, as smart as Brook Mill Stables, but everything seemed bigger and there was a definite atmosphere about the place. After a circuit, Blueberry felt Lucy take up the reins and ask him to concentrate and even though he was excited and delighted to be where he was, at a competition at last, the little brown horse couldn't help feeling something new. It was a strange, fluttering sensation in his stomach and it seemed to be spreading up towards his back and down towards his knees and on to his toes. What if the people didn't like him? What, he thought in a flash of insecurity he hadn't felt in a long time, remembering the big liver chestnut horse which everyone had seen before him, what if they thought he was *too small*?

He felt Lucy's legs close around his sides and they entered the white boards. This was when he had to concentrate and do his best, Blueberry remembered. It was when he was within the white boards, laid out in a rectangle with letters spaced around just as they were in the indoor and outdoor arenas at Brook Mill, that he was always asked to concentrate one hundred percent.

Walking, trotting, cantering, moving as straight as he could along the centre line, making transitions – Blueberry did everything Lucy asked him as well as he could. Going past the side of the arena where all the people

68

were sitting was a test of his concentration. He had been ridden in the indoor school at Brook Mill with people sitting along the sides, so he wasn't particularly worried about that, but he was aware that these people were the ones who were looking keenly at his performance and he didn't know which ones were awarding him marks for everything he did. Maybe they all were! Would his marks be high or would they mark him down, he wondered fleetingly, before concentrating again on what Lucy was asking him to do.

The test didn't seem very complicated – it was just walking, trotting and cantering around, with a serpentine in trot and a walk on a free rein (which Blueberry remembered to do perfectly), and Blueberry didn't find it very difficult. It crossed his mind that if he thought it was quite easy then maybe he wasn't trying hard enough, maybe he was missing something! It was only difficult because he was being watched – but even that didn't really faze Blueberry as he found he was enjoying having an audience. It somehow made all his schooling worthwhile.

Lucy asked him to halt. Blueberry stood proud, his legs square, his ears forward. He felt Lucy pat him and ask him to walk off on a loose rein so he could stretch his neck and relax – his first dressage test was over! Blueberry heard a buzz in the gallery from his audience. Was it an appreciate buzz or where they wondering what the little brown horse was doing here, competing against all the more experienced horses? Was it a good buzz or a bad buzz? Blueberry lifted his head and looked across at them all as Lucy asked him once again to halt. Would he ever know?

As Lucy and Blueberry stood in the arena, a man stood up and started talking to all the other people there. It was a few moments before Blueberry realised that the man was talking about him – about his dressage test. Pricking his ears he heard the man say some nice things about his test, and he seemed particularly impressed by his big canter. The man talked about the marks he would give Blueberry for each part of his test. Was this, thought Blueberry, how all dressage tests were marked? Did the judge stand up and tell everyone, so that everyone could hear what he did well and what he did badly? It was quite intense, Blueberry thought, wondering how Orange had reacted to it, and knowing he would have hated it.

After only a few minutes, Lucy picked up the reins again and asked Blueberry to leave the school, and they passed another horse coming in to the school for its test. Lydia was outside with a treat and Blueberry's rug, which she threw over his quarters.

"Well done Blueberry, you were terrific," she told him, and she and Lucy made a huge fuss of him, which he appreciated. He must have done okay, after all! Dismounting, Lucy disappeared to catch up with Carl and discuss Blueberry's performance – Carl had been in the gallery watching from a safe distance. He had been delighted with Blueberry, pleased with the way he had taken everything in his stride and had managed to concentrate well. The remarks after the test had been particularly encouraging. This first outing had been a huge success for the little brown horse. Carl frowned as he remembered the bigger, chestnut horse's performance earlier. Orange had been nervous away from the familiar surroundings of home, and had found it difficult to concentrate on his rider's requests. The two horses were so different, thought Carl. But that was the point of these early outings, to introduce the horses to the unfamiliar. Blueberry seemed totally at home, even though he was away from home!

The two horses were soon untacked and in the horsebox heading for home.

"I'm so glad that's over," said Orange, too upset to eat his hay. "All those people staring, having my performance analysed afterwards. I hope we don't go to many of those." He shuddered, remembering his experience.

"I can't wait to go to another one," said Blueberry, tucking into his haynet with relish. "Did you really not enjoy it? I was a bit worried at first but, actually, I think I like an audience, it's great to know people are watching me and (I so, so hope) appreciating what I can do. I want to go to lots of competitions!"

"You're a strange little horse, aren't you?" said Orange. Blueberry didn't know how to reply to that, especially as Orange had mentioned the L word and called him little.

"We haven't got any rosettes," Orange said, "so we can't have done very well. Most of the horses come back with those. We've got nothing."

Blueberry's heart sank. It was true; they hadn't seen any rosettes being offered. He knew the successful horses at Brook Mill always came home with brightly-coloured ribbons fluttering in the horsebox cab. He and Orange were totally rosette-less.

"I understand you and Orange have been on an outing," said Lulu, sitting down outside Blueberry's stable door later that evening and keeping her one eye on things around the yard.

"Oh Lulu, there you are!" cried Blueberry, stretching his head down. "I looked for you this morning because I didn't know what was happening and wanted to ask you. But it was wonderful! Lucy asked me to perform some movements in front of some people who seemed to mark us. I think they liked us."

"Judges," said Lulu, noticing a few sparrows pecking up hay seeds outside a corner stable. "It's the judges who dish out the marks, it's the judges you need to impress, they're the ones who can make you or break you, kiddo. Make sure you know which humans are the judges – because it's no good trying to impress the wrong people. It has been done. It's a total waste of time and energy, trying to impress the wrong people."

"How will I be able to recognise the judges?" asked Blueberry. He knew Lulu liked nothing less than wasting time and energy, especially when it was her time and energy being wasted.

"They hang out in little sheds, usually. At least they do if your test is outside," Lulu told him, yawning, "like they're hiding. They call them judging boxes but they're sheds all the same. Shifty people, judges – they like to see you, but they don't like you to see them."

It had been a busy day for the little dog what with all the smells she'd had to identify, the farrier she'd needed to keep an eye on and a big delivery of feed to supervise, not to mention the postman to watch out for. Usually the postman delivered things – parcels and letters and important papers – that kind of thing, but Lulu found it difficult to believe that someone would only ever be so generous as to always *give* something. She couldn't help be suspicious and was waiting for the day when he tried to take something, instead. And when that day came she would be ready…

"Sheds?" said Blueberry, confused. "There weren't any sheds there today. I would have noticed."

"That's because it was inside. Plus it wasn't a real competition," said Lulu, casually. "You went to a judges' seminar."

Blueberry looked blank as he felt his heart sink. He'd been sure he and Orange had gone to a competition. He wondered what Orange would say when he knew they hadn't.

Lulu continued. "It's to train judges, to keep them up-to-speed. You were a guinea-pig, you and Orange, together with all the other horses. It's a good way of getting you out and about, used to the competitive atmosphere and all that. Carl likes to introduce his horses to the hustle and bustle of competitions without putting too much pressure on them in the early stages. It's very important."

Blueberry's chin wobbled like a jelly, trying to understand what his friend was telling him. Why did judges have to be speedy? What was a guinea-pig? He did understand what she meant by a competitive atmosphere as riding at the competition – no, he corrected himself, *judges' seminar* – had been very different from riding in the arena at Brook Mill. He was disappointed that it hadn't been a real competition. After all, it had felt real enough but that, he supposed, had been the point. And then something else occurred to him.

"So, if it wasn't a competition," he said, slowly, "is that why we didn't get any rosettes?"

"Of course," Lulu told him. "Although, of course, rosettes aren't guaranteed, you know. Only the top horses win rosettes. Lots of horses win nothing at all."

"Well anyway," said the little brown horse, feeling much better about their lack of rosettes, "I wore my mane in plaits and Lucy was all dressed up in a black jacket and white stock. I felt very smart and I really think it helped to lift my performance. Isn't that odd?"

"Never underestimate the value of window dressing, kiddo," Lulu replied and hearing Carl call from the house the two magic words that were *Lulu* and *dinner*, sped off to ensure Willow didn't eat her share.

Whatever does *window dressing* mean, wondered Blueberry, realising that the more he learned, the less he seemed to understand.

He couldn't wait to go to a proper competition. 'When would Carl let him prove himself?' he asked himself. He decided that whenever that happened, he would try so hard Carl would enter him for as many competitions as he possibly could. He just hoped he wouldn't have to wait too long for his chance.

Chapter twelve

It was only a few days after the competition-that-wasn't-really-a-competition that Lydia tacked up Blueberry and led him out of his stable to the mounting block where she gathered up the reins and mounted, sitting gently down on his back and finding her off-side stirrup.

"Looking forward to your hack today?" Lydia asked him, giving the little brown horse a pat on his gleaming neck. Blueberry snorted his answer.

He always looked forward to a hack! Blueberry loved hacking. Riding around the beautiful Gloucestershire countryside was a great way to pass the time and all the horses at Carl's yard hacked out regularly. Today, however, instead of being joined by Orange, or Uthopia or any of the other horses Blueberry usually hacked out with, he saw Regency ridden by one of Carl's pupils, Angela, waiting by the gate. Regency's white blaze glowed in the bright sunlight but, when Blueberry and Lydia drew level with the bay and his rider, Blueberry could see that the bay's feelings about going for a hack were about as far away from his own as possible.

"Aren't we going in the school?" Regency asked, as Angela asked him to walk beside Blueberry. The two girls began to talk, confident their mounts would walk on briskly, as keen as they were to explore the countryside.

"We're going hacking," said Blueberry, sneaking a mouthful of leaves from a hedge. Even hacking didn't make him forget food completely. Lydia never had the heart to tell him off, even though it wasn't considered well-mannered. Carl's philosophy was that hacking should be enjoyable, rather than work.

"What's hacking?" asked Regency.

Blueberry felt his chin wobble. How could anyone not know what hacking was? Perhaps

Regency didn't know that's what riding out in the countryside was called. Blueberry explained. "It's a great way to get exercise," he said, "and sometimes we see squirrels and rabbits or even deer, and everything is much more relaxed than schooling. Hacking is great, you'll love it!" He didn't tell him how the squirrels made Orange jump or how his friend snorted at the rabbits and leapt at the sight of deer. No need to suggest problems.

"I don't think I will love it," Regency replied, as he slowed down and shortened his neck, bringing his chin closer to his chest. His eyes widened as he looked around him at all the open fields. Open fields again! They made him feel very nervous. He wasn't used to it. Feeling her mount slow, Angela closed her legs around his sides, asking him to walk on. She felt the horse under her lift his head and drop his nose and her contact with his mouth through the reins was lost. As soon as he felt the reins loosen that mere fraction Regency stopped and whipped around so he was facing the way he had come, then he jogged up and down, keen to return to the safety of the yard.

Blueberry's ears whirled around like a windmill. Where had Regency gone? One minute he was up beside him, the next he was heading off back to the yard with Angela doing

79

all she could to stop him. He felt Lydia swivel in the saddle and look back in amazement as she asked Blueberry to halt.

A few moments later Regency appeared again, with one of the Brook Mill grooms at his head, leading him back to Blueberry.

"I didn't think he'd be nappy" said Angela, shaking her head. "He's so good in the school, the perfect gentleman."

"I don't … want… to… go… hacking!" said Regency, through gritted teeth. "I don't like it out here!"

Blueberry remembered Regency's despair in the field. He just couldn't cope with open spaces and was genuinely scared of being outside. It went way beyond just being naughty or obstinate; he found the whole experience terrifying. Blueberry longed to tell Lydia about Regency's phobia, for that was surely what it was – but of course he couldn't. He needn't have worried though, for she knew all about it.

"Carl thought his problems were just about being turned out in the field," Blueberry heard Lydia say to Angela, "but it seems that his troubles are much worse than we thought. He only feels safe when he's in his stable or being ridden in a school or arena because that is all he's used to. Poor horse."

"Carl thought some of Blueberry's confidence might rub off on him," Angela replied, "but that doesn't seem to be happening. If his neck gets any shorter, I'll be holding the bit rings."

Knowing that Regency would try the same trick of getting behind the bit again so he could whip around and head for home, Angela was being very aware of her rein contact. Even though Regency found it impossible to turn around, and had to obey his rider because she held him between her legs and her hands, he was clearly very unhappy about it.

"Won't you just give hacking a try?" Blueberry asked him, anxious to help. Seeing Regency's distress made him forget to snatch at the hedges and the tall grass, which was unheard of – everyone knew that Blueberry liked to mix hacking with snacking. "I mean, I'm here so you're not alone, and Lydia and Angela are really nice, they won't tell you off or anything, and they'll make sure nothing bad happens to you. Look, we're almost at the woods, isn't it great? Look at all the sunlight pouring through the leaves like spotlights." Blueberry loved walking though the woods on a sunny day. The shafts of sunlight which fell through the leaf canopy like lasers always made him think of The Silver Dancer, illuminated at night by different coloured lights. Blueberry always thought that hacking through the woods was like walking through nature's laser-light show and he liked to imagine that he looked like The Silver Dancer, only lit by sunbeam spotlights. The light didn't have the same effect on poor Regency.

"What are all those bars?" he asked, his voice quivering.

"What bars?" asked Blueberry, mystified.

"Those white bars. This place is like a cage, a big, wide, open cage!" cried Regency. "Or are they spears, or arrows? Are we going to be pierced by hundreds of spears?"

Blueberry realised his hacking companion meant the sunbeams. Where he saw beautiful laser-lights which lifted his soul, Regency saw only danger, which caused him to panic. 'How could patterns made by the sun through the trees mean such different things to them both?' wondered Blueberry. His heart sank. Poor Regency saw the world in a completely different way to himself. Perhaps that was a bit like how his good friend Orange felt, only more extreme. Blueberry began to understand a little more about Orange's fears and sympathised with him. What if he, Blueberry, saw danger wherever he looked? How scary his life would be, and how exhausting.

The sight of the sunbeams was too much for Regency. Coming to an abrupt halt, going

82

against all his training and ignoring his rider, he stood on the edge of the woods and trembled all over. No matter how much Angela encouraged him with words and pats, no matter that Lydia steered Blueberry into the woods along the path away from him, thinking Regency would follow rather than be left on his own, the bay horse with the blaze was paralysed with fear and nothing would entice him to move his quivering legs. It was only when Angela, realising their plans for a hack were proving too traumatic for her mount, asked him to turn back toward Brook Mill that Regency shot forward and hurried back to the safety of the yard, a bemused Blueberry walking along behind him.

Blueberry didn't miss his hack out – Angela saddled the dark brown mare Honeysuckle and rode out with them after all – but Blueberry couldn't get his mind away from the image of Regency looking fearfully at all the sunbeams in the woods. Listening to Lydia and Angela talking, he gathered that his former companion had only ever been ridden in the school or outdoor arena and so, just as his reaction in the field suggested, had no experience of life outside. Even as a foal and a youngster, it appeared he had been kept in a barn, with little or no time in a field. Blueberry felt very sad and couldn't enjoy his hack out like he normally did. It felt wrong for him to be enjoying himself when Regency had been so miserable – even though he imagined he was happy again now he was back in his stable. He wanted so much to help him. Blueberry decided he would ask Lulu about it. She was bound to have some ideas about how he could help his new friend.

Chapter thirteen

"**H**e's agoraphobic," said Lulu, matter-of-factly. "Agoraphobia is a fear of outside spaces. It's unbelievable to you and me but, sadly, the condition does exist. He's not the first horse we've had here who has suffered from it, but I must say he's got it bad."

"What causes it?" asked Blueberry. If he knew the cause, maybe he could help Regency.

"Well in Regency's case, as was the case with the other horse we had here with the same problem, it was caused by the owners treating their horses like toys."

Lulu could see that Blueberry didn't understand her, which was hardly surprising.

"Let me explain," said Lulu, answering Blueberry's prayer. "There are some people out there who want a horse but are not keen on all the work keeping a horse entails. They want to ride it, but they don't want to ride out on hacks, they just want lessons on it and to improve their own riding. They don't mind brushing and playing with its mane and tail but they don't want it to get dirty, and they don't want to brush the dirt off from their horse and get it on themselves. Are you with me so far?"

Blueberry nodded. He didn't understand why there were people who didn't want to do those things, but he believed Lulu when she said they existed.

"So, they get a horse but they only ride inside, where it's warm and dry, and they have their lessons because that's what's important to them. And they keep their horse in a stable and never turn it out in the field where it can get dirty – because again, it's important to them for it to be clean because dirty horses mean hard work. But horses don't like that kind of life."

"Regency does," Blueberry interrupted her.

"That's because that's the only life he's ever known and so it's messed with his head. He's not *happy* because he's not doing what's important to horses – eating grass, playing, running around and hacking out with their mates. He lives a solitary life in isolation. You could say he's a prisoner, but a willing one at that. He's so used to his un-horsey life he panics when he's faced with the life he should have, the life he was born to have. He's been conditioned – and it's wrong. Wrong, wrong, wrong!" Lulu said, getting quite angry. She was angry not only for Regency, but for all the other horses who were not allowed to live as natural a life as possible. She was also angry because she knew some people treated their dogs the same way, causing all sorts of behavioural problems. She and the other dogs at Brook Mill were allowed to roam the yard and fields all day, which she loved. There was always so much to sniff at and people around to throw a ball or pass the time of day with.

"How can we help him?" asked Blueberry, unaware of Lulu's wandering thoughts.

"I'm not sure we can, it sounds as though he's too far gone to help," Lulu sighed. "It's sweet of you to want to, but I think he may be a hopeless case. Carl will keep trying of course; he won't give up on him. It makes him cross when he sees the result of some people's selfishness. People who mess with animals' minds need a stiff talking to, or worse. I'd like to get tough with them; I think it's the only way sometimes. You have to be tough to do some good. The things some people do to dogs and horses are just …," Lulu took a deep breath and pulled herself together. "Sorry kiddo, but it makes me mad! They'd be better off with one of those mechanical horses."

"I know Carl wants to help Regency," said Blueberry, who didn't know anything about mechanical horses, but didn't really want to go off the point by asking about them. "He thinks he can be helped, I know it!"

"I'm sure you're right," agreed Lulu. "Maybe we need to give it more thought. If Carl thinks Regency can be helped to live the life of a normal horse then it could be possible. We'll get our thinking caps on."

Blueberry thought about what Lulu said. He tried to sleep but his thoughts kept returning to Regency and his man-made problems. He wished he had a thinking cap. He wondered what Lulu's thinking cap looked like. Maybe he could borrow it – she must know he didn't have one of his own. Where did you get a thinking cap? He didn't like to ask her. Sometimes, when he asked her things, she just snorted as though she was stifling a laugh, although he didn't know what could possibly be funny.

The little dog's words went around and around in his head. Sometimes, Blueberry knew, his best ideas came to him when he was asleep. It was as though his mind worked things out when he wasn't trying too hard, and it took over when he was resting and found solutions for him. As he drifted in and out of sleep Blueberry's brain formed all kind of ideas. When he woke up the next day he kept hearing Lulu's voice saying, *'You have to be tough to do some good,'* over and over again. He couldn't help thinking that was the key to helping Regency. The trouble was, he didn't know how.

Chapter fourteen

Sitting in his office in his house by the stable yard, looking out of the window past The Silver Dancer and over to the field where Blueberry, Uthopia and Orange grazed, Carl ignored the paperwork on his desk as his mind wandered. Carl planned the dressage careers of all his horses very carefully. It was vital that they looked forward to their lessons, that they had a good life-work balance with schooling, hacking and field time, and that every horse in his care and under his training reached their full potential – in whichever direction that might take.

Blueberry, the little brown horse he had almost sold on before realising his mistake, excited him. Not only was he well-built and confident, but he seemed to love his work, and that was important. When a horse enjoys learning, and loves to give the rider that which is asked, teaching and schooling are a joy, Carl knew that. Some horses took longer than others to learn how to adjust to their riders' requests, but Blueberry was a quick learner. When he rode him, Carl could feel the little horse trying his hardest, asking; 'Do you want me to do this? Or perhaps this? Or maybe this? Should I do it this way? Or is this better? Or would you rather I did this?' His enthusiasm was second to none – and it rubbed off on his rider. It was infectious.

It was a shame, thought Carl, that Blueberry was always going to be a little too small to make a competition horse on which he himself could compete. True, he was riding and schooling him now – together with other pupils and students, and Lucy, of course – but Carl and Blueberry didn't make a very compatible pair. Carl was too tall and Blueberry too small for the partnership to present a totally elegant picture to any dressage judge. It was such a shame, Carl thought, as he would love to compete with Blueberry at top competitions in future. He might even – and it was early days yet, but the little horse's potential shone out – make a really top class dressage horse. Were future Olympic Games totally out of the question? Carl didn't think so. The horse was an exciting prospect, but deep down Carl knew he wouldn't be the one who would take him to the top.

Carl thought hard. Was there anyone on the yard, any of his students or pupils who might do this little horse justice in competition? Lucy was great, he acknowledged, but she wasn't going to stay at Brook Mill. She had plans of her own regarding her own future. No, Carl decided, there was no-one currently at his yard who might make a match with Blueberry. He would have to keep looking.

Carl wasn't too worried. It was early days in the little brown horse's career and Carl knew that patience often provided the right solution to a challenge. The important thing was to get the right partnership, the right pairing. Rushing could result in the wrong rider for his star equine pupil and Carl was determined not to make that mistake. He would know the right rider for Blueberry when he saw them – he just had to keep his eyes open. He and Lucy could introduce Blueberry to his early competitions until that magic person came along. When they did appear, they and Blueberry would continue on their journey together, forging a partnership built on trust, empathy and ambition. It would happen, Carl knew. He knew because he was determined to make it happen.

And then there was Orange, thought Carl, leaning forward in his chair and wondering whether he would have to run out of the house to stop Willow chasing the guinea-fowl. He could see the row of birds nervously making their way along the side of the outdoor arena, looking around for danger, but Willow hadn't seen them yet. Carl sat back as Willow made his way away from the arena to the feed store, leaving the guinea-fowl to wander around in peace. His thoughts returned to Orange.

The big chestnut horse had talent, too. He had good paces, he was impressive to watch – but he lacked his friend Blueberry's courage. Blueberry was a 'going-towards' horse; whenever he saw something new he was curious, wanting to check it out and explore. Blueberry saw the world as a wonderful, exciting place, full of new things to discover. Orange, on the other hand, was definitely a 'going-away' horse. Whenever he saw something unfamiliar he was instantly suspicious. The world according to Orange was full of bogeymen and things which were out to get him. Anything new needed to be run away from before it could do him harm.

Orange's ancestors were true survivors – running away and fleeing anything unusual before it could eat them. It had stood them in good stead in the wild, where the difference between being relaxed and being suspicious often meant the difference between being eaten and living to flee another day, but for a dressage horse it was a definite handicap. There were so many new things to discover, so much going on in the world. That the big chestnut horse was getting better and more used to the unusual lifted Carl's spirits. He hated to think of Orange being nervous – he liked his horses to be chilled and enjoy life. Like Blueberry, Orange showed talent as a top dressage horse and Carl hoped that given time he would realise that nothing was going to harm him, so he could enjoy his life and career more.

Every horse on the yard was different, Carl acknowledged. That was partly what made working with horses so fascinating and thrilling. He would never know everything about horses – nobody would. There was always another horse which taught him something new, another horse which challenged him. And with that in mind, Carl's thoughts turned to Regency, the horse he had in for schooling, the horse which had real problems – man-made problems – which Carl was determined to solve. Orange's hiccups were minor compared to those of the agoraphobic horse. Carl frowned as he put his mind to some serious, Regency-themed ideas, unaware that Blueberry was giving the problem his attention, too. There had to be a way of helping the bay, he thought. There just had to be.

Chapter fifteen

The next day, when Blueberry was turned out in the field after his schooling session, the weather had changed dramatically. Instead of sunshine, dark clouds whizzed overhead, driven by high winds. Instead of kicking up dust from the grass under his hooves, he and Orange slipped on mud where the clouds had hurled down water in the night. Not put off by the damp and mud, Blueberry still rolled

96

enthusiastically, but when he stood up and shook from his nose to his tail the mud clung to his coat and sank even deeper into his mane and tail.

"You look terrible," said Orange, "even though the mud is the same colour as your coat."

"You look worse," replied Blueberry. "You're the same colour as me, now. You're more acorn than orange!"

"Here comes the rain again," said Orange. "We'll be back to our own colour soon."

The horses didn't mind the rain. It wasn't cold and the water was refreshing. It did, however, make them kick up their heels and gallop around the field, throwing up mud in all directions.

"Oh look," cried Orange in surprise, "it's Regency."

They both stared as Lydia opened the gate and led the reluctant bay through. Every muscle in the bay's body screamed against being let out in the field with Blueberry and Orange but Lydia undid his headcollar, closed the gate and stood back anyway. Lulu had been right; Carl wasn't going to give up on the agoraphobic horse.

Blueberry trotted up and sniffed noses with the newcomer. "Come and play with us," he said. "It's great fun in the rain."

Regency stood rooted to the spot where Lydia had left him, his eyes showing his fear of being out in the open.

"Come on," said Orange. "Don't be such a buzz-kill."

"Honestly, it's all right," said Blueberry, aware of Regency's terror. "Just try it, take a few steps." But the bay refused to move, neighing to be taken back in.

"Why do they keep putting me out here?" Regency wailed. "They know I hate it. I want to stay in my stable!"

"Well, you could try it for a little longer," Blueberry suggested, trying to be sympathetic. "I know it's raining, but you can still have some fun with us."

"Fun?" asked Regency. "Fun? Are you trying to be funny? How can I have fun in this… this… place? It's so dirty out here! So open! So wide!"

"You're even more of a wuss than I am," said Orange, "you need to toughen up a bit."

You have to be tough…

Blueberry blinked as those words went around his mind again and he took a deep breath and a leap of faith. "Come on Regency, you're coming into the field with us!" he cried, diving behind him and nipping the bay's quarters. Regency squealed and took a step into the field in surprise.

"What do you think you're doing?" he said, glaring at Blueberry.

"Yes, what *are* you doing?" hissed Orange, amazed at his friend. He had never done anything like it before and Orange was shocked.

"Move, Regency," ordered Blueberry, nipping Regency's flank.

Outraged, the bay moved another three steps forward. "How dare you!" he cried, turning around to face Blueberry. "If this is how you treat your guests…"

"I'm just warming up," said Blueberry, whirling around to get behind Regency again. "Come on, move it, shift your rump you lazy thing!"

"Have you gone mad?" whispered Orange.

"No, help me get him away from the gate – by whatever means possible. It's for his own good," Blueberry whispered back. Performing the equivalent of an equine shrug, Orange joined in and the pair of them hustled Regency away from the gate and into the middle of the field. Blueberry saw Lydia out of the corner of his eye as she rushed towards the gate, intent on taking the visitor away from his unfriendly and downright hostile companions. She was amazed to see her normally nice-natured charges ganging-up on the innocent Regency. She had to rescue him from them!

But she was too late. Without even realising how he got there, Regency suddenly found himself a long way from the safety of the gate, right out in the middle of an open space with only Blueberry and Orange next to him, nipping and shoving him further and further away from his perceived safety.

"I'm soaking wet!" spluttered the bay. "And my legs are all muddy. I can feel the mud getting into my hooves."

"Great, isn't it!" said Blueberry, shaking himself so that droplets of water and mud went in all directions – including all over Regency.

"I'm going back to the gate!" Regency announced, whirling on his hind legs in a perfect pirouette and cantering off. Blueberry and Orange galloped after him, one on either side in order to dictate the direction so that the three of them galloped around in a semi-circle and came back to the centre of the field, much to Lydia's dismay. Deciding she would have to get all three horses in, she ran back to the yard for help. By the time she returned with two other grooms and Carl, her frantic story of Blueberry and Orange ganging up on Regency had changed somewhat.

"They look like they're playing to me," said Carl, folding his arms and grinning, despite the weather. Regency, the formerly unhappy, agoraphobic horse was cantering around with his two new friends. All three were covered in mud and ignoring the rain which lashed down. It had taken Blueberry getting tough with the bay to prise him away from the fence but miraculously, once Regency had found himself in the middle of the field, and had discovered the joy of galloping, bucking and playing with Blueberry and Orange, he remembered how to be a horse and forgot to be scared. Blueberry had shocked him out of his comfort zone and allowed him to discover how he could enjoy being outside.

Carl was thrilled. He had wracked his brains to find a solution to Regency's problem without coming up with much. It seemed that in this case, his horses had done the work – and Carl couldn't help thinking that the intelligent little brown horse known as Blueberry had played a big part in it all. Regency would always have problems but he was on the road to becoming a horse again, a horse which could carry out his normal behaviours in the field instead of being stuck in a stable twenty-four-seven. Now, thought Carl, he and the rest of the staff at Brook Mill would carry on where Blueberry and Orange left off.

"Is rolling in the field really fun?" asked Regency, doubtfully, as he watched Blueberry go down on one side and thrash about in glee.

"Why don't you try it?" suggested Orange. So Regency did. Grunting with unaccustomed effort, he sank to his knees and felt the mud on his back for the first time, rolling over and over to smother himself completely and then leaping up, bucking with joy.

"I understand our visitor has had a breakthrough," Lulu said to Blueberry that evening, giving him an enquiring look.

"That's right, he was very brave," Blueberry told her.

"I can't help thinking you had something to do with it," said Lulu.

"Actually, Lulu, it was your idea," said Blueberry.

"Mine? Really? Well it doesn't surprise me," his friend replied, coolly. "Err, which idea of mine was it exactly?" she added, in a voice which suggested she wasn't too bothered if he didn't tell her. Blueberry knew better.

"Oh, well really it was my idea *based* on one of yours," Blueberry told her. And that was all he said. It made a change, thought Blueberry, to be mysterious and keep Lulu guessing. Besides, he felt awkward telling her about how he and Orange had forced Regency away from the gate. It felt a bit like he was being big-headed.

"But I didn't know whether the idea would work or not. I'm only glad it did. I love going out in the field so much, and enjoy hacking out that I can't imagine not being allowed to do either. I just wanted Regency to know how it could feel, and to enjoy it, too," Blueberry explained.

Lulu looked at her friend. She knew the little horse was intelligent, she knew he was smart but she hadn't, until now, realised just how kind he was. Not everyone has the ability to put themselves in another person's shoes – or, in this case, another horse's hooves – but it seemed that Blueberry did. Not only that, he wanted to help his new friend and lots of people, and horses, wouldn't have bothered. Blueberry's actions had helped an unhappy horse. More importantly, Lulu thought, they told her a lot about Blueberry. She had been right about this horse, Lulu decided, she and Carl.

"Well I'm glad it worked," she told him. "Good job, Blueberry!"

Chapter sixteen

Ever since his first outing to the judge's seminar, Blueberry had been desperate to go to a real competition. He didn't have long to wait. Only a few days after Regency discovered how to gallop and roll outside in the field, the little brown horse's mane was plaited once more and he was led up into the horsebox. On this occasion his travelling companion was Uthopia, the almost black stallion, a year older, and therefore more advanced in his schooling than Blueberry. This time, Blueberry sensed, he was off to a real competition – there was just something about the way Lydia seemed more excited which, in turn, made Blueberry excited. What made it even more special was that Lulu came too. Knowing this was a big day for Blueberry, the little dog had jumped up into the cab and refused to budge, even when Carl asked her to.

"You really want to come?" Carl had asked her, sensing when her mind was made up. "Okay then, but be good, no nosing around the other horseboxes for dog treats!"

Lulu decided that if checking out the horsebox park was going to be part of her day's agenda (highly likely, she thought), she would make sure it took place when Carl was riding or watching the competition. She didn't want to scupper any chances of being allowed on future outings. Blueberry didn't realise Lulu was a member of the party until they arrived at their destination and she bounded up the ramp to meet him as Lydia led him down and onto the grass.

"Time to prove yourself, kiddo!" Lulu barked, which made Blueberry feel slightly pressured. This feeling left him, however, when he looked around and saw just what a vast event they had come to. There were some big white tents and signs and horseboxes and cars all parked in the field. Humans wearing tabards were directing everyone. There were more tents which looked like shops selling lots of saddlery and clothing for humans and horses, dressage arenas marked out on the grass as well as a big indoor school in the distance, and far too many dogs on leads to count. There were lots of nice and not-so-nice smells of cooking, sounds of people shouting, laughing and loudspeakers crackling into life and keeping everyone up-to-speed with what was going on, and calling competitors for their classes. It seemed to Blueberry that nobody could possibly know what was going on, at what time, and where – but it seemed that everyone did.

"Wow, Lulu," Blueberry breathed, forgetting even to drop his head to graze, "this is an awesome place. It's much bigger than the last event."

"I told you, last time wasn't a competition. This is a big one – but don't worry, because you're entered for the Badminton Young Dressage Horse of the Future class, so nobody expects too much from you. The test is a very simple one just to show off your paces and training so far. It's restricted to four- and five-year-old horses so you'll be against horses a year older than you are, including Uti. Don't get too stressed about it, it would be unusual for a four-year-old to beat the five-year-olds. You're here for the experience."

Blueberry gulped. Even if nobody expected too much from him, he had high expectations of himself. This was his chance to prove that he was a top dressage horse in the making, and he vowed not to blow it. Even though he was putting pressure on himself, despite Lulu's advice, the little horse was so interested in what was going on all around him his chin forgot to wobble. Lydia plaited his last two plaits at the bottom of his neck and Lucy soon appeared in her black jacket, polished long boots and stock. Carl was already on Uthopia, warming up. Uti looked very calm and composed, very professional, thought Blueberry, hoping he looked the same. He felt a pang of disappointment. If only Carl was riding him! He must think more of Uti, thought Blueberry, than he does of me. Of course, he reminded himself, Uti had been to lots of competitions whereas this was his first real one. Despite this, Blueberry allowed himself to dream of winning a rosette. Could that be possible? Did dressage horses ever do that at their first show? He felt guilty for wishing Carl was in his saddle when he liked Lucy so much, and he vowed to try his heart out for her.

Warming up here was nothing like warming up at the judge's seminar. Here Blueberry walked and trotted around with lots of different horses and, he noticed, ponies, too. As he and Lucy tried to concentrate on achieving relaxed yet controlled paces, Blueberry heard snatches of the other horses' conversations.

"I wish these Pony Clubbers weren't here, getting in our way," said a snooty-looking chestnut.

"Very distracting!" agreed a dappled grey.

"You needn't be so up yourself!" cried a dun pony with a plaited tail and a tall, thin girl in its saddle. "Someone has to train up the dressage riders of the future. They're not born with the ability to ride you warmbloods, you know!"

"You tell 'em, Ricky!" exclaimed a chubby piebald with a Spanish plait along its neck. "Don't look down your long nose at us!"

"At least some ponies have the look of a dressage horse," continued the dappled grey, glancing at Blueberry. "Isn't your rider a bit old to be in the Pony Club?"

Blueberry realised the dappled grey was talking to him. "I'm not in the Pony Club competition," he said, breathlessly. "I'm entered for the Young Dressage Horse of the Future."

The dappled grey stifled a giggle and looked across at the rangy chestnut.

108

"Yes, of course you are dear," sniffed the chestnut. "And I'm a stalwart of the British Olympic Dressage Team!"

"Oh, you are a scream!" said the dappled grey. "We might believe titch here when he grows another hand or two!" he added. "But honestly, Young Dressage Horse of the Future? You must think we came down with the last shower of rain to believe that!"

The chestnut and dappled grey laughed, leaving Blueberry with a total confidence crisis. How could those horses think he was in the Pony Club competition? It was his lack of height, he thought, his heart sinking. They'd judged him purely by his size. After all his training with Carl, surely they were able to see past his lack of inches? What did he have to do to prove he was up to the job? He had felt so like he belonged here but now, after hearing the other horse's comments, Blueberry almost wished he could go home to Brook Mill. Was that one of the reasons why Carl was riding Uti and not him? The little brown horse put even more effort into his paces.

"How does he feel?" Carl asked Lucy as they rode around, each avoiding the other in their warm up.

"It's like sitting on a rubber ball," Lucy told him. "He's excited and bouncy – I don't think

I'll have any worries about impulsion!" she laughed. "He is listening to me, even though this is all new to him so he should be all right," she added.

Little did Blueberry know that even though Carl needed to concentrate on Uti, there was still a part of him which wished he could ride Blueberry. But Carl had faith in Lucy and knew she would do a brilliant job in Blueberry's first real competition. The Badminton Young Dressage Horse of the Future was a great way to measure the little horse's training against all the young potential dressage horses in the country. Although Carl had no doubts about entering Blueberry, despite his young age and small stature, he still wondered what the top international judge would think of his little brown horse. Blueberry had grown, it was true, but he was still the smallest horse on his yard and he was a distinct shape, not the usual stamp in competitions.

The farrier, when he shod Blueberry, always called him Bob-the-cob, in reference to his stocky build. The little brown horse always felt slightly insulted when he heard him say this, although he didn't quite know why. He had no idea what a cob was, he just knew the farrier never referred to any of the other horses by the same nickname. Lulu had insisted it was a

110

compliment but Blueberry had the feeling she was just being kind. Now, with the spiteful comments of the other horses ringing in his ears Blueberry realised he was still seen as small, still seen as a horse which was at a disadvantage in the dressage arena.

"I'll just have to try harder," Blueberry vowed, determined to prove the other horses wrong. But even so he could feel his chin starting to twitch. He hoped he could control his nerves.

Lulu sat next to Lydia, watching Blueberry. She sometimes went to competitions and she had seen plenty of young horses at the beginning of their dressage careers but there was something about Blueberry at this, his first major event, which she hadn't seen before. Was it that he seemed excited? Most young horses at their first competition seemed to shrink in stature and poise as they were surrounded by all the more experienced horses around them. Was it that he was concentrating on his rider, as well as tipping an ear in Carl's direction whenever he spoke? She had seen first-timers so distracted by all the sights and sounds at a competition that they couldn't concentrate on their riders at all. Or was it that the little brown horse seemed totally dedicated to the job he had to do, remembering his lessons and working as well as he possibly could, even in his warm up? Even experienced horses sometimes forgot lessons learnt with all the excitement of a showground. But then, suddenly, Lulu noticed her friend's chin wobbling. He was worried about something. What could it be?

"What do you think, Lulu?" Lydia asked the little tan dog, patting her head but never taking her eyes off Blueberry. "How do you think our boy will do today, against all this stiff competition here?"

Lulu's confidence in the little brown horse in front of her wavered. Up until she had seen the wobbling chin, she hadn't thought Lydia – or anyone else – had anything to worry about. But now she wasn't so sure…

Chapter seventeen

It was time; time for Blueberry's first real dressage test, his first time in the spotlight. Lucy steered him around the snowy-white boards and Blueberry looked around. The indoor arena was big, bigger than the one at home, with flowers decorating the sides and there were quite a number of people at the top end. It was quite intimidating what with all the colour, faces and whispers from the crowd. No sheds, he noticed, because he was inside. So where was the judge, or judges? They must be amongst the people watching and it was the judges he had to impress, Blueberry remembered. It was the judges who decided the score, not the crowd watching. Nor, Blueberry suddenly realised, the other horses who thought he was headed for the Pony Club dressage competition. How dare they! This was a defining moment for Blueberry. Now was the time to prove to everyone he was capable of following his dream to be a top dressage horse. Now was the time to put those comments behind him and put all his effort into remembering his training, into listening to Lucy, to performing the best dressage test he could!

As he and Lucy entered the dressage arena within the boards, a hush descended on the crowd. Blueberry had always wondered how it would feel to perform in front of people and now he was actually going to do so. He didn't feel scared. He no longer had a confidence crisis. Now, he couldn't wait to show them all what he could do. With his heart thudding in his chest, Blueberry began his test.

Lulu had been right, Lucy only asked him to do some of the movements and paces he had practised at home – only this time Blueberry, buoyed up by the people watching him and desperate to prove himself, tried even harder to impress them. He wanted them to know that he,

Blueberry, was the new kid on the block, one he was determined they would remember. The test was over too soon for Blueberry and he couldn't believe it when Lucy asked him to halt and she saluted. His rider had only asked him for walk, trot and canter on both reins, plus an extended trot along the long side of the arena, but he had put his all into the movements.

Stretching his neck, Blueberry looked around at everyone. He hoped he had done well – he thought he must have because people were clapping. He recognised that sound; Carl often asked everyone on the yard to come around the arena or into the indoor school and applaud so that the horses got used to it.

Someone stood up and said something, but Blueberry was so busy looking around he didn't really take much notice of the words except when he heard the man say how impressed he was with this horse's canter. He pricked his ears and looked at the man. Could he possibly be talking about him? It was too late to listen, the man had come to the end of his speech and Lucy steered her mount out of the arena and back to the waiting horsebox.

"Nice work, kiddo," Lulu told him as Lucy slid from his back and Lydia took the reins, giving him lots of fuss and telling him how clever he was. Did she mean that, Blueberry wondered, or was she just saying it to make him feel better? He felt his confidence melt away. Maybe he hadn't done enough to win a ribbon. Maybe the judges hadn't liked what they saw. Maybe his canter was the only part they had liked. There was no way he could tell – except that Blueberry was sure Lulu wouldn't say anything unless she meant it. He could always rely on his friend for the truth, he realised, as insecurities about his test crowded his mind. He hadn't realised he would feel like this. Not only did he think once again about the mistake his fellow horses had made regarding his height, but he wondered how he would measure up against the five-year-olds who had been training for a whole year more than he. How could he possibly compete against Uti? Blueberry's euphoria had been short-lived and now his mind was in a spin. And then his old nightmare returned; if he didn't do well, would Carl send him away again?

Blueberry took a long drink and stood, suddenly tired – not from the physical effort, but from all the thoughts whirling around his head – as Lydia threw a light rug over him. He had performed the best test he could, he decided, but the competition was fierce and there were plenty of good horses competing against him, not to mention Carl on Uthopia. Blueberry knew it was unlikely that a young horse, the horse that was so small in stature and cobby-looking against the other horses, could perform as well as the others, no matter how impressive his canter might be.

It wasn't long before Uti returned with Carl, who was beaming from ear-to-ear.

"I'm so pleased with him," Carl said, patting Uti as his gleaming black boots hit the ground. He and Lucy went off to see the other tests being ridden, leaving Blueberry and Uti to talk with Lulu about how they thought they had done.

"I couldn't have done any more," said Uti, looking confident. "And I know Carl was happy with my work. Quite a crowd today – how did you get on, Blueberry?"

"I'm not sure," Blueberry replied. "I think I did okay – Lucy seemed pleased."

"He did great," interrupted Lulu. "He just hasn't got anything to measure his performance against yet, this being his first real show."

"Well, we'll find out soon enough," sighed Uti, as Lydia replaced his bridle with a headcollar and made a fuss of him.

"I'll go and see what's happening," said Lulu, forgetting about her plan to search for dog treats and scuttling after Carl and Lucy who were waiting for the scores to be announced.

"You see, this is how it works in a dressage competition," explained Uthopia, as Lydia made

117

the horsebox ready for their return journey. "We each get a score for every movement we make – a transition from walk to trot, for example, or that trot along the long side of the arena."

Blueberry nodded. He remembered Lulu telling him that and had realised how important every single movement was. Just messing up one or two could make a difference between a high overall mark and a low one. Good, consistent scores were needed, Lulu had told him. Not high for some and low for others, hoping the high ones would pull up the score. It would be more likely that the low ones would drag down the highs, she had explained. They all had to be the best they could possibly be, the highest scores they could achieve for each and every movement. That was why Carl was so particular about each horse's schooling. Every horse on his yard was schooled to do everything as well as they possibly could, rather than relying on what they did best.

"So once the judge or judges have given you their score or scores these are written down on what's called your test sheet, and all the individual scores are added up to make a total. It's this total which give you your overall score," continued Uti, who was grateful to have Blueberry to talk to, giving him something to take his mind off the result yet to be announced.

He, like Blueberry, had done his very best and tried his heart out and was anxious to know whether the judges had liked what they had seen.

"I think, though," continued Uti, "that this competition for the Badminton Young Dressage Horse of the Future is slightly different, if I remember from last year. You heard the judge speaking about our scores at the end of our tests? Well the five horses with the highest scores are asked to go back in the arena and trot around together for another mark for s*tar appeal*, awarded according to how much star quality the judge thinks each horse has, and then the overall winner is announced."

Blueberry hadn't realised that the person who had stood up after he had finished his test had been speaking about his scores. Why hadn't he paid attention! How long would it be before they knew whether they had done enough to be in the top five best horses? He hadn't thought he might have to do more – if he was selected for the final five, of course. The competition seemed to be taking ages and ages. While he waited his mind galloped on, his insecurities returning to race around his head. He had never been plagued by doubt before. The little brown horse had always believed in himself, believed in Carl. How could he feel like this at his first show? The negative comments of the other horses had affected him more than he realised

Both horses lifted their heads when they heard Carl and Lucy coming back and Lulu raced ahead of them, her tongue lolling outside her mouth as she came to a hurried stop by the horsebox.

"Hey kiddo!" she cried, between pants. "You'll never guess what!"

Blueberry's chin went on a spree. He was last. He had terrible marks. His dreams of being a dressage horse were over even before they'd begun. Carl would be disappointed in him and he was going to have to re-think his entire life and career.

"Both you and Uti are in the top five!" barked Lulu.

The little horse froze. Lulu was joking. It was a cruel joke, Blueberry thought, his heart sinking as he wondered how she could do such a thing. But he should never have doubted his friend.

"Both boys are in the final judging," Carl shouted across to Lydia, who whooped and jumped up and down like a mad person, causing a big bay horse which was warming up nearby to shy and snort. Lucy threw her arms around Blueberry's neck and gave him a hug. Blueberry's ears plopped forward in shock and he glanced across at Uti who was just as pleased for both of them. Lulu jumped up and down, barking.

Going back into the arena for the final judging was more nerve-wracking for Blueberry than his first test. Now there was more at stake. All five horses showed off their paces for the judge and Blueberry, aware of how important this final judging stage was, put his all into his performance, taking great care to perform his very best. This was his chance to show everyone that he deserved his place in the final, whatever his final placing, his chance to silence his equine critics who had dismissed him as too small. But how could he win against the five-year-olds, he, the little horse mistaken for a pony?

Lots of spectators had crowded into the arena, impatient to see who would win the Badminton Young Dressage Horse of the Future. Would the victor go on to greater things? Would they witness history in the making? Or would the winner be a horse which was good now, but didn't possess the ability to go further, to work its way up the dressage ladder and be the very best, maybe the best the world had ever seen?

The loudspeaker crackled, making Blueberry jump. A voice boomed out, telling everyone that the winner of the Badminton Young Dressage Horse of the Future this year was…

Blueberry felt Lucy crumple in his saddle and heard a sob escape her. So, they hadn't won, they hadn't done as well as they had hoped. But then he realised that the name he was hearing over the loudspeaker, was his. Not Blueberry, his stable name, but Valegro, his registered name, his *professional* name. And the person was telling everyone that he, Valegro, was the winner. He couldn't understand why Lucy was upset – he thought she'd be pleased.

It appeared that Lucy could be upset even when she was thrilled and Blueberry wondered whether he would ever stop learning things!

Chapter eighteen

That evening, telling Orange all about his first real competition, Blueberry relived every moment. The test, the crowds, the rosettes he had won and the shimmering victory sash which had been fastened around his neck, declaring to everyone that he, Valegro, was the Badminton Young Dressage Horse of the

Future for that year. Orange listened and *oohed* and *ahhhed* in all the right places, happy for his friend and even happier that he hadn't gone to the show. It sounded too traumatic to him – all those people, all that pressure! When Lulu arrived, she added her version to the story, and by the time that Blueberry and Lulu were too tired to speak any more, Orange was fully up-to-speed with all the day's events.

"Were there really lots of people watching?" Orange asked, thinking how much he would have hated it.

"Masses!" said Blueberry, remembering how it felt when they all clapped and cheered as he and Lucy had cantered around the arena in front of all the other horses, in front of Uthopia and Carl who had finished in second place, in front of the dappled grey horse which had been so rude to him. The dappled grey hadn't looked so superior then, Blueberry remembered. Rosettes had fluttered from his bridle and he had heard the clicking of the photographers' cameras over the sound of music from the loudspeakers. Winning a competition had felt even better than he had imagined it might – better even than in his dreams. He felt pride and joy and satisfaction in his work all at the same time. He had loved the crowds applauding him – it was so thrilling. He couldn't wait to go to another show and do his best again.

When darkness fell over Brook Mill, signalling the end of Blueberry's first day of competition and his unexpected success, the little brown horse lay down in his stable, his excitement giving way to sleepiness. He could hear Lulu's rhythmic breathing as she lay curled up under his manger, already fast asleep. It had been a long day for her, too.

I hope I don't wake up tomorrow and discover this has all been a dream, thought Blueberry, his eyelids closing. The thought occurred to him that now his dressage career had really begun – not just begun, but had taken off like a rocket! He was following in the very first hoof beats of The Silver Dancer. Now he knew how it felt to be a winner. Now he understood how wonderful being a dressage horse was and he longed to have that feeling again and again. Now, Blueberry thought as he drifted off into a deep sleep, he had to make sure he did the same thing in every competition he was entered for. He would do his very best, and climb as high in the dressage world as he possibly could. How high could he go? Blueberry was determined to find out.

If you enjoyed reading this book you may want to answer these questions or discuss them with your friends or class:

Chapter 1

'If you don't do them perfectly, You. Will. Mess. Up.' What effect does the author create by using one word sentences?

Do you think Blueberry likes his stable? What part of chapter one makes you think this?

Chapter 2

Why doesn't Blueberry think that the training is arduous?

Lulu refers to Blueberry as her 'pupil', what does that tell you about Lulu?

Chapter 3

Why was it important to Carl that his horses were kept *'happy and far from dull'*?

What does the author mean by *'sniff-a-thon'*?

Chapter 4

Why does Lulu think it's good that some of the dogs end up with a *'horsey home'*?

Brook Mill is home to many animals, what does this tell you about Carl?

Chapter 5

Why are Blueberry's hindquarters referred to as the engine? What is the author trying to convey?

What had the weather been like just before Carl took Blueberry outside the arena for part of his lesson?

Chapter 6

Blueberry is keen to befriend Regency. Do you imagine that Orange would be equally keen?

Were you surprised that Orange couldn't imagine how they could help Regency overcome his fear? If not, why not?

Chapter 7

We learn a lot about Blueberry's attitude to work in this chapter. If he were human, do you think Blueberry would enjoy school? What subjects do you think he'd be particularly good at?

Carl wants his horses to be prepared for potential distractions at competitions. What do you imagine these distractions might be?

Chapter 8

'Blueberry wished he could get to know them better. He felt sure that if Lydia liked them, they weren't as superior in manner as they appeared.' What does this tell us about Blueberry's opinion of Lydia?

What does the phrase *'nought-to-sixty'* mean?

Chapter 9

What do you imagine the *solarium* is? Why would Carl have one in his yard?

Why do you think Lydia is so keen for Blueberry to stand still while she plaits his mane?

Chapter 10

'It was a big arena but there were some jumps set up inside, which had to be avoided.' Why do you think the jumps were there?

Do you think Blueberry would have performed differently if he had actually known Carl was at the event, watching him?

Chapter 11

Do you think Lulu would rather have been at the competition with Blueberry and Orange than at the yard all day? Can you explain why?

Blueberry doesn't understand the phrase *window dressing*. What do you think it means, how would you explain it to him?

Chapter 12

Do you agree with Carl's philosophy that *'hacking should be enjoyable, rather than work'*?

'One minute he was up beside him, the next he was heading off back to the yard with Angela doing all she could to stop him.' Just what could Angela do to try and stop Regency?

Chapter 13

'People who mess with animals' minds need a stiff talking to, or worse.' What do you think Lulu means when she says *'or worse'*?

What do you think should happen to *'People who mess with animals' minds'*?

Chapter 14

How do you think Carl feels, accepting that he and Blueberry would not make a compatible pair for top dressage events?

The author says *'Orange's ancestors were true survivors.'* Do you think Blueberry's character would have made him a good survivor in the wild?

Chapter 15

Why did Lydia think she would have to get all three horses in from the field?

Both Carl and Lulu appear surprised and impressed by the way Blueberry helped Regency. Do you imagine Orange was equally surprised?

Chapter 16

Why do you think Lulu was so determined to be at the competition with Blueberry?

What is the significance of the fact Blueberry forgot *'even to drop his head to graze'*?

Chapter 17

From what you've learnt about Blueberry so far, which move do you think he would have scored particularly high with?

Do you think the little brown horse would rather be called Blueberry or Valegro? Can you explain your answer?

Chapter 18

This chapter tells us about Blueberry's emotions on that special day. Which aspect do you think was the most important to him?

In chapter one, Lulu says *'When the roof goes on, kiddo, you'll know you've made it as a top dressage horse.'* What do you think Lulu would be saying to Blueberry now?

Blueberry extras

At Brook Mill I insist that everyone mounts their horse from a mounting block, rather than trying to mount from the ground. Pulling on the saddle can twist the seat and this in turn can hurt a horse's back. I also make sure nobody ever holds the cantle (at the back) as they mount, as this can weaken the saddle. Instead, I ask them to put their right hand on the other side of the saddle and remind them to always sit down gently – it's only polite! I'd advise everyone to take care when mounting as this can help keep their horse or pony's back healthy.

I make sure all the horses are checked regularly for any signs of muscular strain so we can pinpoint what's causing it and correct anything before it gets serious. Damage to one side of a horse's back can cause them to move crookedly, so it is vital to make sure everything is even on both sides. And if there is evidence of muscular problems on one side we look at not only the saddle, but the rider! Horses mirror their riders so it makes sense that if the rider sits crookedly it shows up in the way the horse moves. It's attention to details like these which is so important at a top dressage yard, but there's no reason why you can't borrow some of the ideas we have to improve your own riding, and keep your horse or pony in good health.

Good conformation is essential for top equine athletes. That a horse is put together well means he can perform to the best of his ability. Dressage horses are not all built the same – some are tall with long legs and others, like Blueberry, are shorter and more stocky – but the rules of conformation remain for all types of horses. From the side their body and legs should fit roughly into an imaginary square, and this will mean they are in proportion. A short back gives a horse strength to carry a rider and propel themselves forward, and strong hindquarters are where the engine is based. All horses should drive themselves forward from the back legs (rather than pull themselves along by their front legs), so strong hocks and joints – knees and fetlocks – take a lot of strain and need to be sound. A deep chest means the horse has plenty of heart room – a strong heart is essential for stamina and allows the horse to work easily. Legs should be straight. Imagine running on legs which are bowed, or knock-kneed – the strain on one side of the legs will be more than

133

on the other, which means the horse could suffer from injury, as well as knocking himself.

Conformational faults such as a ewe neck (where the top of the neck dips in the middle, rather than arching gracefully) or a thick gullet (thickness in the underside of the neck and jaw) will mean the horse will find it difficult to arch his neck, and may set up problems in other areas. All this is taken into account when people look for and buy a horse for any discipline, and I do the same when looking for a dressage horse. Conformational faults can't be corrected so it's important that the horse is built well to enable him to work properly and, of course, happily.

A plaited mane streamlines a horse and gives it polish. It's an equine up-do, essential for parties! Plait fashions come and go: years ago it used to be fashionable to have lots of tiny plaits fastened with white tape but nowadays we sew in as few plaits as possible to give a neat, unfussy appearance. Blueberry usually has nine plaits along his neck, plus his forelock. They are always sewn in with thread which matches his mane, to give a really smooth look. You don't want a judge to be mesmerised by horrific plaits when they should be looking at the horse's performance! To get neat plaits, you need a short mane and Blueberry's mane is trimmed in order to shorten and thin the hair – just a few hairs when he is groomed every day, so he hardly notices.

Blueberry's tail, on the other hand, although kept neat and trimmed at the dock, is left quite long – it reaches almost to the ground – and is never plaited but left loose. Blueberry's groom is incredibly fussy about his plaits; a wobble in the plait line will make it look as though Blueberry's neck is wonky. If one isn't quite right it comes out and is re-done until they are all perfect. This doesn't happen often because the grooms get so much practice! They need to be tight enough so that they don't unravel, but they also need to be comfortable so that Blueberry doesn't try to rub them, or they distract him when he's working.

Practice makes perfect so if you want great plaits you need to have some dry-runs first! If your pony tries to rub out his plaits then maybe there is a hair pulling or you have put them in too tight. Blueberry is always plaited on the morning of his competition, never the night before, to ensure they are perfect. Not only may your pony try to rub out plaits overnight, but his mane will suffer if it is plaited for too long. Oh, and when you cut the thread to undo them, take care not to cut the mane!

Bonnie and Clyde are Brook Mill's resident cats. They came to us as tiny feral kittens (which means that although they are domestic cats, they were born in the wild so were not used to people). Over the years they've become friendlier and friendlier (Bonnie is *especially* friendly when anyone has a chicken sandwich to share!) but although they interact with the staff and other animals, they still sometimes hear the call of the wild and both of them like to disappear on their own adventures. Clyde interacts more than Bonnie, who is more independent of the two. Even so, Clyde went through a stage of being chased by the dogs and one day he disappeared and didn't come back to us for over a month. Then he turned up looking healthy and quite pleased with himself, so we knew he'd been looked after. He didn't seem at all aware of how worried everyone at Brook Mill had been about him! Now he goes off on his forays quite regularly and we suspect he may have adopted another family part-time. Such are cats – they truly are free spirits.

All the tack at Brook Mill is cleaned regularly – and by that I mean after every ride. Yes, really! We use everyday tack for schooling and hacking out – the competition tack is kept for best although of course each horse wears it at home before a competition to make sure it's comfortable and the correct fit. When schooling Blueberry's legs are bandaged or he wears brushing boots in case he knocks a joint when he tries too hard, and he has overreach boots on his front hooves, to protect his heels. His canter is so energetic, and his strides are so long, we don't like to take a chance on him catching a front heel with a hind hoof. Such a simple slip-up could keep a superstar out of work for a long time – all the horses wear the same equipment to ensure they don't risk injury in this way. There really is no room for taking chances.

All the saddle cloths, bandages and rugs are washed regularly, too. We have a big washing machine and dryer on the yard to cope with all the equine laundry. Keeping saddle cloths clean is particularly important as any build-up of sweat can cause pressure points which in turn can injure a horse's back. A saddle cloth may look clean and fluffy on the upper side but it's the underside, next to the horse's skin, where you need to check. I like to put on clean clothes so I don't expect my horses to wear dirty saddle cloths and rugs!

Schooling sessions at Brook Mill are kept short, and the horses are not schooled (or worked) every day. It is the quality of a schooling session which counts, not the length. In fact, the longer you school, the less likely it is that your horse or pony will learn anything – apart from how boring schooling can be. Schooling is tiring for horses and they can only concentrate for a short time – just like us. If your horse or pony isn't quite getting what you are asking him to do resist the temptation to carry on asking and asking, hoping the penny will drop. It won't and you (and your pony) will get frustrated. When riders get frustrated they can lose their temper – and I don't believe it is EVER acceptable to lose your temper with a horse or pony. If your pony doesn't understand what you want him to do, you need to make sure you are asking him the right way. Losing your temper is the quickest way to make a horse lose confidence in you and you may never rebuild the trust that is lost. It is better to go away and do something else – go for a hack or turn your pony out in the field to relax. The chances are, the next time you are schooling your pony will offer what you asked for, as sometimes everyone needs time for a lesson to sink in. Switching off is a valuable tool – and often a lesson has been learnt, it is the rider who hasn't understood how clever their horse is!

Watch your pony's ears when you ride for they tell you what he is concentrating on. Are his ears pointing towards something in the distance? Then he isn't listening to you, but giving something else his full attention. Are his ears flat back against his neck? He's unhappy, or in pain and you have an opportunity to find out why. Maybe another pony is too close. Maybe he doesn't understand what you are asking him to do, or you are asking him in a rough manner, or maybe his tack is hurting him, or he feels pain in his mouth or his back – perhaps you've been schooling for too long. When your pony's ears are relaxing to either side of his neck it generally means that your pony is listening to you, and what your aids are asking him to do. This is the perfect time to ask for a little more, or to teach him something different for this is when he is concentrating on you.

In this story, Regency was a horse which had never been allowed to be a horse. I believe all horses need time to graze and get dirty in the field, mix with their equine friends and enjoy hacking out. Imagine if you were kept in your bedroom all the time, and only let out for a lesson in maths or science! All our horses at Brook Mill enjoy a life-work balance, and it not only keeps them happy, but gives them lots of confidence. Even if your pony is a mud-wallower, let him spend as much time in the field with his friends as he can. He'll be happier for it, and you should find he is happier in his work for you, too.

When you first start riding, you need to do quite a lot of work to get a horse or pony to do what you want them to do but when your riding progresses you can refine your aids. Instead of doing a lot of work, see how *little* you need to do in order to get your pony to do something. Horses and ponies are sensitive – they can feel a fly on their flank – so they can feel every move you make in the saddle, every breath you take, every slight movement of your arms and legs. If you give lots of aids, or nag with your legs, your horse of pony will switch off, thinking you are just fidgeting. Your signals will become white noise. Instead, sit still, be calm, be aware of every breath and movement your body makes. Turn down your conversation with your pony from a shout to a whisper. Over time you will only need to *think* what you want for your brain to send tiny signals to your muscles and your pony will follow your lead. Try it!

Glossary of equestrian terms

Behind the bit

When a horse or pony is pulling its head towards its chest so the rider loses contact with the bit through the reins

Bit

A metal or synthetic narrow bar, most often jointed, that fits in a horse or pony's mouth attached by rings each side to the bridle and reins

Breeches

A type of riding trouser (or jodhpur) specifically designed to make the rider more comfortable and be worn with tall riding boots

Brushing boots

Boots that are used during exercise to protect the lower leg from injury that may occur if one leg or hoof strikes the opposite leg

Cob

A stocky, rather sturdily built small horse, that often looks like a large pony

Dappled grey (colour)

A grey or white coloured horse or pony with darker ring-like markings called 'dapples'

Dun (colour)

Yellowish or tan coat with a darker-coloured mane, tail and lower legs and a dark 'dorsal' stripe along its spine

Equine Physiotherapist

Physiotherapy for horses can be used alongside veterinary care to help in the treatment or long-term care of many muscular injuries and conditions

Farrier

A specialist in the care of horses' and ponies' hooves, including trimming, balancing and shoeing

Hand (measurement)

A measurement of the height of a horse. Originally taken from the size of a grown man's hand but now standardised to four inches. The measurement is taken from the ground to the withers. It is normally expressed in hands plus additional inches, so 15.3 hands ("fifteen-three") would be fifteen times four inches, plus three inches – that is, 63 inches (160 cm). Abbreviated "hh" for "hands high" or simply "h". The European system of measuring is said simply in centimetres

Liver chestnut (colour)
A coat colour which is a dark brown shade with the same, or sometimes slightly lighter, coloured mane and tail

Masseuse
A masseuse is someone who gives massage therapy to people or horses professionally. Massages for horses can help with overall performance, mobility and range of motion

Nappy
When a horse or pony is 'nappy' he refuses to do as the rider asks, for example refusing to leave other horses, refusing to go forward, bucking, rearing

Off-side
The right side of a horse or pony (the left side is called the 'near') for example: the off-fore refers to the horse or pony's front leg on the right

Passage

Dressage movement in which the horse trots in an extremely collected and animated manner

Piaffe

Dressage movement in which the horse performs a very collected trot on the spot

Piebald (colour)

A horse or pony with patches of black and white colouring

Quarters

Also called the hindquarters, the part of the horse or pony's body above the hind legs from hip to tail

Serpentine

A schooling movement in several loops that involves half circles along the long side of the arena followed by straight lines with a change of direction in between. When crossing the centre line the horse's body should be parallel to the short side

Shy

When a horse or pony suddenly moves back or away from a frightening object

Spanish plait

A plait for a horse or pony that has a very long mane, running along the crest of the neck in one continuous plait

Stock (tie)

A traditional white or cream tie worn around the rider's neck when at a show

Warmblood

A type of horse with at least five generations of recognised sport horse bloodlines, and that has been inspected and registered by world-recognised breeding associations to excel in the sports of dressage and/or show jumping